Praise for

What Do You Want From Me?

"The title of Jennifer Dupree's novel *What Do You Want From Me?* is the book itself in miniature—a slightly aggrieved, subtly funny question from a person who feels obliged, but not happily so. As Maeve struggles, not always successfully to be a good parent, she confronts her own role in the betrayal around which her parents' marriage formed, even as Alzheimer's changes the terms of the decades-old conflict. I loved this novel's sharp writing, clever perceptions, deft characterization, and wisdom about parenting (and coping) in the present moment."

—Debra Spark, author of *Discipline* and *Unknown Caller*

"*What Do You Want From Me?* is a powder keg of infidelity, betrayal, and family secrets, threatening to blow at every delicious turn. Dupree's tender humor and control of language spark and flash on each page. The shrapnel from this story cuts straight to the heart."

—Dave Patterson, author of *Soon the Light Will Be Perfect*

"In her second novel, Jennifer Dupree boldly examines the dynamics of the complicated relationships between mother and daughter, child and parent, husband and wife. Dupree's sly observations both belie and underscore the long-lasting, damaging effects of generational trauma and a lifetime of secrets—often known, and yet kept silent."

—Shannon Bowring, author of *The Road to Dalton* and *Where the Forest Meets the River*

What Do You Want from Me?

What Do You Want from Me?

Jennifer Dupree

Apprentice
House Press
Loyola University Maryland

First Edition

Casebook ISBN: 978-1-62720-608-2
Paperback ISBN: 978-1-62720-609-9
Ebook ISBN: 978-1-62720-610-5

Library of Congress Control Number: 2025931868

Design by Niki Ignacio
Promotional Development by Maggie O'Donnell

Published by Apprentice House Press

Apprentice
House Press
Loyola University Maryland

Loyola University Maryland
4501 N. Charles Street, Baltimore, MD 21210
410.617.5265
www.ApprenticeHouse.com
info@ApprenticeHouse.com

for Nonny

1

Maeve is stringing doughnuts from the ceiling. She has already taken off her pirate hat and eye patch, in part because Paige said it looked "inane" and in part because her eye was sweating and she couldn't see, plus the impediment was causing her to move at a sloth's pace and Paige reminded her six times that her friends would be here any minute.

Peter hands her her cell, which she didn't hear ring because Paige turned up some techno music. Maeve asked her to turn it down. Twenty minutes ago, Maeve asked, "Why not 'Thriller?'" and Paige rolled her heavily-lined eyes.

"Because the 80s were three decades ago," Paige said. Her version of a witch, apparently, goes heavy on the makeup.

It's Maeve's father on the phone. He says, "I don't know what happened but Anita's at the bottom of the stairs." He sounds out of breath, as though he's just run to grab the phone, although Maeve can't think of the last time she saw her father run, if ever.

"What stairs?" Is all Maeve can think to say. It's been years since Maeve heard her father say Anita's name and for a moment all Maeve can picture is Anita from thirty years ago, and in this version, she's sitting cross-legged at the bottom of the stairs, holding Clipper, laughing. But then Maeve registers the panic in her father's voice and she knows that whatever has happened is bad. "Is she hurt?" Maeve asks. Peter is gesturing with a bottle of Sprite and Maeve can't really focus on what her father is saying.

It's eight o'clock and her father is likely well into his Captain's and Coke by now.

He says, "The ambulance is on the way. You need to come and stay with your mother."

Peter gestures that he's going to pour the Sprite into the punch and Maeve nods. She asks, "What happened?" Her breath feels like a dozen balloons let loose over a parade. Her father sounds afraid and Maeve can't ever remember him ever being anything except defiant, even in an emergency.

Her father takes a shaky breath. "Anita was coming up from the basement stairs and she fell. It doesn't matter, Maeve. Are you coming?"

He doesn't bother explaining why Anita was at the house to begin with, which means he assumes Maeve can figure it out.

Through the phone, Maeve hears the sirens. Her father says, "I don't want to leave your mother alone."

"Why—?" She's thinking *broken arm*. She's thinking *twisted ankle*.

"I called next door but Collette must be out." Her father breathes into the phone. His voice is muffled, but she can hear him tell Effie it's all right, everything will be all right. He sounds as unnerved as he sounded the day Clipper got hit by a car.

Paige's friends have begun to arrive, each of them letting in a blast of cold air behind them. While Paige finishes cutting olives to look like horns on deviled eggs, Maeve opens and closes the door, over and over again, and waves them in. There's a girl in white pajamas with a unicorn horn on her head, a boy with curlers in his hair and an apron around his waist, someone taller than everyone else in a Donald Trump mask Maeve finds disconcerting, especially when the kid points at her and drawls "You're Fired." Maeve has not yet finished hanging the doughnuts although she's trying to. She tucks the phone between her ear and shoulder and reaches up with a strung doughnut. But her phone is too thin and slippery and it clatters to the floor. When she bends to retrieve it, the doughnut brushes the carpet. Maeve wonders if it really matters—these kids have hearty immune systems and probably consume a lot worse than a few bits of dirt—but, Paige is watching her, so she throws the doughnut away, string and all.

The plan is for Paige and her friends to eat the doughnuts with their hands tied behind their backs. The first one to eat an entire doughnut gets a box of orange-sprinkled doughnuts, which Maeve realizes is grossly redundant.

Into the phone, Maeve says, "I'm in the middle of Paige's party."

Peter has put on a Farrah Fawcett wig he got from who knows where. How is that not "inane?" There's no way Paige's friends even know who Farrah Fawcett is, unless they've seen re-runs of Charlie's Angels, which Maeve doubts, and the whole thing is only funny because it's Peter, wearing a wig. Peter's high-fiving the kids and handing them cans of Silly String. Maeve had no idea he purchased Silly String, but he's exactly the kind of person who would. When Maeve finds Paige, she's ready to commiserate about how her father has embarrassed her, but Paige is holding a mayonnaise-y egg in one hand, an uncapped can of Silly String in the other. She looks delighted.

She hears the door of her parents' house open, the heavy thud of work boots. "I need to go," her father says. "It's—they're loading her in the ambulance."

Even after all these years, he's choosing Anita.

Maeve jams her feet into Paige's boots because they're the ones next to the door and Paige doesn't need them right now. Maeve finds her car keys under a pile of mini-Snickers. On her way out the door, Maeve asks Peter to keep an eye on the doughnut eating contest and the kids in general. He frowns and asks if everything is all right and she says no, not really, she'll explain later—she'll call. Peter gestures to the spot where her eye patch was and says "aye, aye." She waves apologetically to Paige, who shrugs and straightens her witch hat which makes Maeve realize how short her black dress is.

Maeve drives as quickly as possible through the murky night full of witches carrying pumpkins and holding the hands of ninjas and zombies. Once, when Maeve was six or seven, her mother sewed her a costume of grapes, each felt grape stuffed with cotton and then attached to a purple leotard, She topped Maeve off with a knit purple cap and a felt leaf. Maeve loved how cocooned she felt in that costume.

When Maeve was thirteen, Anita Haverland bought her the most outrageously ornate fairy wings—huge, glittery things Maeve wanted but couldn't afford. Anita did her makeup that night, an elaborate eye makeup that everyone at Stacy Ambrose's Halloween party said was the best they'd ever seen.

By the time Maeve gets to the pale-yellow split-level on Evergreen that she and Stewart have always referred to as the Ever-yellow, the ambulance is gone and her mother is eating chunks of cheese from a block that has gone green at the edges, fuzzed in the center.

She tugs off her boots. Effie looks up and smiles. "When

did you get in?"

Maeve kisses her cheek. "Just now. What happened?"

Effie holds up the cheese. "Do you want some?"

The house hums with the energy of an emergency just gone by, but Effie seems to have forgotten it, or to never have noticed it to begin with. Maeve takes a knife and shaves off the moldiest bits of cheese. How has her father let the cheese mold? He can't still be relying on Effie to take care of things around the house. She sets the kettle on for tea, then tries her father's cell to see if he can tell her more about what happened with Anita. It goes straight to voicemail.

Kids keep ringing the doorbell and Effie keeps getting up to answer it. Maeve follows her to make sure she's not opening the door to anyone who looks dangerous, but of course, tonight that's everyone. Peter texts Maeve to ask where the rug cleaner is and she texts back a series of question marks. They've never owned a rug cleaner, although she rented one last spring. Why is she the only one who knows this?

When the kettle boils, Maeve sets the bowl of candy on the porch. Someone might take the whole bowl, but they might not. She dunks the teabag twice for her mother's tea, adds three teaspoons of sugar and an ice cube before putting it in front of her.

Maeve leaves her mother with her tea and navigates the poorly lit stairs that lead to the dim laundry and storage area in the basement. What would have made Anita come down here? There, at the bottom of the stairs, is a Rorschach test in blood. Maeve sees a flower, a butterfly, a clown. She'd thought, when her father called to say Anita fell, that she's sprained an ankle or banged her knee. This looks like more blood than you'd get from a knee, but Maeve can't be sure.

Upstairs, Maeve sits across from her mother and sips her tea.

Maeve says, "It must have been a bad fall."

"Who?"

"Did she hit her head?" Maeve doesn't really expect a coherent answer, but she doesn't know how to talk to her mother except in the way she's always talked to her.

"Cracked like an egg," Effie says.

Maeve blinks at her mother. She seems...delighted.

"I know you don't like Anita, Mom, but it sounds like she's pretty badly injured."

Effie stares out the window, her lips drawn into a hard line. It's possible Effie has already lost the thread of their conversation, or maybe she just doesn't want to talk about an affair that has—it seems—gone on for decades.

"I hope she's going to be okay," Maeve says.

Effie makes a raspberry, spitting tea in the process. "You always liked her more than you liked me."

Maeve wipes the counter and her mother's chin with a paper towel. "That's not true, Ma." Tears clog her sinuses.

But Effie is drinking her tea and looking at Maeve like she's just realized Maeve was in front of her. "What's not true?"

*****

Her father finally calls to say that Anita has a head injury, and that it's bad.

"Oh, my god," Maeve says. "How bad? What are the doctors saying?" She doesn't ask what happened or why Anita was at the Ever-yellow. There will be time for that later.

"Not much," he says. "Your mother—"

"I'll bring Ma home with me."

There's a pause and then Tom says, "Thank you."

Maeve hasn't heard him appreciate anything in years and she feels something like gratitude for his gratitude.

Upstairs, Maeve packs her mother's soft flannel pajamas, the ones Maeve bought for her last Christmas. They still feel stiff at the creases, as if they haven't been worn. Maeve has a flash of anger at her father, who has probably been letting her mother go to bed in a t-shirt and his old boxer shorts. She didn't buy the pajamas so they could sit in a drawer, unused. She bought them so her mother could be warm and comfortable. Why can't he manage to make that happen?

She packs her mother's toothbrush, her lavender lotion, her foam curlers, her cold cream.

Back downstairs, Maeve picks up her mother's purse, which is heavier than a purse should be unless it contains several hundred dollars in change. Maeve opens it to find two handfuls of screws and a banana. "What are you doing with all this, Ma?"

Effie looks out the window at the kids—now mostly just the older ones wearing hoodies and dark jeans, some in George Bush masks. "Is there a parade?" Effie asks.

Maeve waits for a break in people before leading her mother to the car. Who knows what Effie might say to someone dressed as the former president.

It's only as they're pulling onto Maeve's street that Maeve realizes she hasn't warned Peter she's bringing her mother home with her. He'll be surprised, but not angry. He'll never say she should have checked with him first. He'll just ask if he needs to change the sheets in the spare room. He'll get her mother clean towels and place them on the bathroom vanity. He'll turn on the nightlight in the hall, which they only ever use when they have guests. Paige will be too preoccupied with her party to care that her grandmother has arrived, unless Effie embarrasses her by asking every kid if she knows them.

Inside, Peter greets her with Silly String dripping from his head. "Hey," he says. He kisses Effie. "This is a nice surprise."

"Mom's staying the night," Maeve says. "Dad's at the hospital."

Peter's face changes from amusement to alarm. "What happened?"

"Not him." Maeve toes off Paige's boots. "It's a long story."

Effie squints at the roomful of teenagers squirting each other with Silly String and—dear God—whipped cream. "Is this Romper Room?" She walks toward the kids, but Maeve takes her arm. "Let's get you washed up, Ma." Over her shoulder, she promises Peter they'll talk later.

After she finally settles her mother into bed, Maeve texts Dr. B to say she has the flu and won't be in tomorrow. He texts back to say he hopes she's better soon.

It's after midnight before the kids all get picked up and Maeve and Peter wipe sticky goo off every surface. "Why did you give them whipped cream?"

Peter shrugs. "They found it in the fridge. I couldn't take away the fun."

He could have, and Maeve doesn't want to be annoyed that he didn't. She says, "Remember how I told you my Dad had an affair when I was a kid?"

"Of course," he says, and she can tell he's trying to listen, but the trash bag he's tying breaks and paper plates, pizza remnants, and doughnut crumbs spill onto the floor. "Shit."

They both clean it up, then bag the rest of the trash.

Maeve ties the bag while Peter sprays Windex on the

counter and scrubs hard. "The affair was with Anita Haverland. And she fell down their basement stairs tonight."

He looks up. "Are they all friends now?"

"I don't think so. I think maybe she and my Dad never stopped seeing each other."

Paper towel still in hand, he gathers Maeve to his chest. He smells like whipped cream and Windex. "That's hard."

She'd like to stay pressed against his chest, but she can see piles of Silly String under the dining room table, in the plant in the corner, on top of the microwave.

When they finally crawl into bed, Peter falls instantly asleep. But Maeve can't sleep. Instead, she sees Anita Haverland—or the Anita Haverland she knew thirty years ago—tumbling down her parents' stairs, the black clip that always held her hair back cracking open and flying into thin air.

2

Maeve is six and Stewart is eight, and they're in the car with Aunt Grace driving and their mother crying in the passenger seat. It isn't snowing, but it snowed yesterday, and their mother hasn't cleared the snow all the way off the car so it feels like they're in a snow cave, which Maeve loves the feel of even though she knows this is not a time to feel comforted.

Aunt Grace says, "Just knock on the door and tell him to come home."

Their mother touches her eyes with her fingertips. "I made a mess of my face."

Aunt Grace has turned off the radio and Maeve wishes she'd turn it back on so that they'd have something to listen to other than the low moan of their mother.

"Remind him he has a family," Aunt Grace says. Her hair is pulled tight on the sides.

Effie says, "He's not going to like that I went after him."

"Too bad," Grace says.

Effie wipes her nose on the sleeve of her beautiful coffee-colored coat, the one Maeve helped her pick out, the one she wasn't going to buy because it cost too much, but Maeve told her she should have beautiful things. Maeve knew better, even then, not to say she'd heard Anita Haverland say that when she was at the Haverland Health office, drawing on white paper with colored highlighters.

Effie says, "As long as I know he's okay. What if there's

been some kind of accident?"

They drive all around the neighborhood behind the school until Aunt Grace stops and backs up. "Didn't you say Neal Street?"

In a small, strange voice Effie says, "There must have been some kind of emergency."

Aunt Grace takes their mother's hand with one of her pretty, pink-nailed hands. She turns down Neal Street, headlights stretched out on the quiet road that leads down to the lake and then down a long, winding dirt driveway that leads to a house that looks like it's made of just logs, stacked neatly on top of one another. If their father is here, he'll for sure know they're coming. Maybe he'll come out onto the porch and wave them in and everything will be fine. Stewart says, "Is he playing poker?"

Neither their mother nor Aunt Grace answers. Maeve inches closer to Stewart and he slides his arm around her. Their father does play poker on some nights, but they've never gone out looking for him before.

Aunt Grace pulls up to the big house with the wraparound deck, the lake just visible beneath the moon. She shuts off the engine. "This it?"

Their mother stares out the window and says nothing.

Stewart reaches for his door. "I can go knock," he says.

Their mother whips around. "Sit down," she says even though they're both sitting.

Their father's truck is in the driveway. A layer of snow dusts the windshield.

Aunt Grace opens her door. Effie says, "It could be something to do with work. It's just strange that he's been gone so long. And no one answered when I called the house."

"Let's find out." Aunt Grace whispers this, but Maeve is right behind her and so she hears. Hears, too, the edge of frustration in her Aunt's voice. She can feel the heat from her breath.

Maeve sneaks a look at Stewart to see if he can figure out what's going on, but he's staring at the house, same as their mother. She can see a light on above the kitchen sink, but nothing else.

Grace opens her car door, gets out, and smooths her blouse so it's tight over her chest. She click-clacks up the walkway and rings the bell. Her back is as straight as a ruler. Someone answers the door, and Effie lets out a little moan. Grace goes in and the door closes behind her and Maeve wonders if she'll disappear forever, like the children in Hansel and Gretel, although in the end they make it out all right. The witch doesn't, and who, in this case, is the witch?

Finally, Grace emerges from the house. She's ramrod straight, her hair in its neat low ponytail just as it was when she went in. Somehow Maeve expected her to be wind-blown. She opens the car door, settles herself in. "He says he told you Charlie's been sick." She starts the car. As she backs out of the driveway, she puts a hand of Effie's knee. "He brought dinner over for Anita. They were eating lo Mein at the counter. Charlie was in the bedroom, resting. He has the flu, that's all."

There's something very bright about the way Aunt Grace says this that makes Maeve think of how she told her mother she didn't know what happened to her Barbie when the truth was Maeve had thrown it down the stairs to see if Barbie could fly. A lie, told with as much cheer as possible for the sake of believability. Barbie broken in three pieces, one arm and one leg broken free, no matter which story you told.

Effie closes her eyes for so long Maeve thinks she's fallen asleep.

Their father comes home that night, after Maeve and Stewart have gone to bed but not before Maeve has fallen all the way to sleep. She hears her father say, "I can't help what you think."

And then her mother, "I know a thing when I see it."

*****

Stewart was named for Jimmy Stewart, because their mother had watched "It's a Wonderful Life" more than thirty times, but she didn't like the name George or Jimmy, and their father said Bailey was a dog's name.

"Just an all-around nice guy," Effie always said when she told about how Stewart got his name. And then she'd kiss Stewart on the cheek or forehead.

Maeve was named for no one. Her mother liked "May" but Maeve was born in June and so could not, according to her mother, be named after a different month.

Peter tells her she puts too much stock in the naming of things, but it took them six days after her birth to settle on Paige's name. "Something with possibility," Maeve said.

"Something functional," Peter said.

*****

It's Grace who brings her mother Clipper. Three days after they all sit in the driveway of Anita Haverland's house, Aunt Grace shows up with Clipper, small and white and trembling. "His owners can't keep him," Grace says.

"Why?" Maeve asks. "Why can't they?"

No one answers her and she pictures two old people dead on the floor, which she knows is from a show she saw her father watching when she was supposed to be in bed. After Maeve cried and cried about the two old dead people, Effie explained they were just actors and not really dead at all. Actors who got up from that bed and washed their faces and went home to their families and dinner and their own soft beds as soon as they were done acting for the day. Still, old dead people is what Maeve thinks of as she looks at the little white dog.

Grace holds him out to Effie and Effie takes him and cradles him against her chest. He looks at Effie like she might be the most wonderful thing he's ever seen. "Clipper is a terrible name," she says. "Maybe we'll change it." But then they start calling him Clipper and, within a day, it seems too late to change it.

3

Paige wears a t-shirt and no jacket and Maeve decides to pretend she doesn't notice that it's twenty degrees out and Paige is shivering. She isn't blue, and Maeve figures that's a good sign. "Start the car," she says. Ten minutes ago, Maeve went up and knocked on Paige's door and asked if she was ready to go driving, and Paige said she wanted to go driving two hours ago and Maeve said she was doing the best she could.

Dinner was ready when she got home, but her mother refused to eat the macaroni and cheese Peter made because she insisted she already ate. Maeve made her mother half an egg-salad sandwich, which Effie ate like she was starving. When she finished, she said she was still hungry, and so Maeve gave her a Yodel and Effie ate that and asked for another.

While her mother ate a second Yodel, she called her father. "She's so confused, Dad. I think she needs to be home."

In the ensuing pause, Maeve could hear the beeps of Anita's machines through the phone. "Can you bring her home and stay with her?" he asks.

"Maybe for a few days. How long do think you'll stay with Anita?"

"She's in pretty bad shape."

Maeve closes her eyes and rests her head on the cool countertop. "I'll just keep Mom here. That'll be easiest. She'll be okay." Maeve isn't sure this is true, but she can't move into her parents' house. It feels like some kind of trap she'd never escape.

At eight-fifteen, after Peter cleaned the kitchen and Maeve was making a to-do list for tomorrow, she remembered she'd promised to take Paige driving.

"I'll take her," Peter said. Which Maeve considered, but knew Paige would hold against her. She kissed him and said, "You've been doing so much already."

He beamed at that, which made Maeve feel bad for all the attention she hadn't been giving him.

It's only when Paige opens the garage door that Maeve realizes it's snowing.

Paige says, "I can't drive in the snow."

The snow is like cotton shaken from a pillow, light and bright against the headlights. "You have to do it eventually."

"But this is only, like, the third time I've ever driven."

"We'll just stick to the neighborhood." Maeve rests her head against the seat. She'd like to close her eyes, but that would be irresponsible.

Paige backs out of the garage, braking too often and jerking the car needlessly. Maeve clamps her mouth shut. They creep down the driveway.

As Paige straightens the car, Maeve says, "I appreciate how much you've been helping me with your grandmother."

Paige shrugs. She slides the car from reverse to drive and then eases her foot onto the gas. A turtle could pass them. Thank god there aren't any other cars on the road.

It's snowing harder now. "Turn left," Maeve says. And then, "Put your windshield wipers on. And your lights."

Paige puts on her left directional, then her right, before finally landing on the switch for the lights. She drives with her hands hard-gripped on the steering wheel. After a few minutes, Paige asks, "Is Grampa in love with Anita?"

"Jesus, Paige. No. He loves your grandmother. Why would you even ask that?" Maeve says this with so much conviction she surprises herself. And even while she's saying it, she knows it isn't true. Her father does love Anita and always has. She's not going to discuss it with her teenage daughter, though.

Paige still doesn't have her windshield wipers on and snow has accumulated like a soft film. Maeve feels like she's entered an alternate reality. If she were not the mother and Paige the teenaged daughter, Maeve would ask her if she thinks it's possible to love one woman for decades and still love the one you're married to. Instead, she says, "Wipers, honey."

Paige glances at Maeve and the car drifts to the right. Maeve tries to hold her door subtly. "There was a lady delivering a package yesterday and Gram got all freaked out that it was 'that woman' and it took me ages to get her to calm down. Anyway, she said something about Anita. It was just weird because she was so worked up."

The roads haven't been salted and Maeve can feel the slide of the tires. "Your grandmother's confused."

They're approaching the stop sign that leads out onto Main and Paige slows the car a bit jerkily. She says, "I know. But she also said that when Anita and Grampa were arguing she was like, backing away from him and that's how she fell. The whole thing is like a soap opera or something."

Maeve can't breathe.

Effie taught Maeve to drive because Tom wouldn't let her out of the driveway until she'd memorized all the hand signals. The only one she could consistently remember was a hand straight out the window meant she wanted to take a left.

Paige keeps driving, both hands on the wheel, staring

straight ahead. Snow splatters the windshield. Paige glances left and the whole car moves left.

Maeve says, "You need your wipers on higher, Paige."

Paige is the same age Maeve was when Anita gave her a camera and taught her about light and contrast. When Maeve would have traded her own mother for Anita in a heartbeat.

They're only going ten miles per hour, past a pretty gray house, straight down Pine St., which will eventually lead them back to Main.

Paige taps her brakes and the car fishtails.

"Easy on the brakes," Maeve says. "My mother and Anita had a complicated relationship."

Paige jerks the wheel and the car turns one full revolution. Maeve waits for the crunch of metal against metal, but nothing comes. Just the slow spin like the end of a carnival ride and the intake of Paige's breath. The car slows to a stop in front of a house Maeve has always liked—small, white with black trim and a cheery red door.

"Oh, god," Paige says. "I'm sorry." She's shaking and Maeve puts a hand on her arm.

"It's okay. We're okay." Maeve feels like her heart is running wild through the rest of her organs. She has a flash of her father's face the day he caught her spying on him and Anita, the fury in his body, the way he moved toward her like he might shove her off the porch.

She and Paige sit in the quiet car for a long time, snow accumulating slowly on the windshield, Maeve wondering if the people in that pretty little house have secrets, too.

*****

That night, while her legs are across Peter's lap and they

watch the ten o'clock news, she says, "Paige said my mother said my father and Anita were arguing when she fell."

Peter pulls his eyes away from the weather forecast and frowns, trying to parse out her sentence. She doesn't want to repeat it, so she's grateful when he nods. "You think your Mom remembers?"

Maeve leans back and closes her eyes. "I don't know. It seems weird that she'd just make that up."

"The brain is tricky." He rubs her legs. She feels herself drifting to sleep. "Your Dad must feel terrible if that's what happened."

"Maybe that's why he won't leave her bedside. Guilt."

He gives her legs a gentle squeeze. "She also doesn't really have anyone else."

Maeve leans her head against the couch cushions. Anita's husband is in a nursing home and Maeve doesn't know if Anita had many friends, besides her father, who was obviously more than that. "I guess that's true."

4

Maeve dreams her mother, in a long black ballgown, tells her Anita Haverland is at the door. But when Maeve goes to the door, there's a giant Jack-in-the-Box on the stoop. Maeve cranks it, even though she's flooded with dread. She cranks and cranks and cranks and the lid creaks and snaps, but never pops, and nothing ever emerges.

Still groggy, Maeve comes down to start the coffee and finds her mother sitting at the kitchen counter with a plate of from-the-freezer waffles in front of her.

"Why are you up?" Maeve asks. Her mother is wearing Maeve's bathrobe, untied, over a pair of knee-high nude stockings and nothing else. Maeve ties the bathrobe's belt so that her mother is at least not entirely exposed.

Effie swats at Maeve's hands and then continues to eat. "Why is that any of your business?"

Maeve sniffs the air. Clean, she thinks.

"Where's Peter?" And then Maeve realizes it's after seven, which means Peter has taken Paige to school and himself to work and Maeve slept through all of it. And Effie wouldn't know, anyway.

These days, her mother never wakes up before eleven—except today, apparently—and she no longer makes herself breakfast. Instead, Flora, who Stewart has hired to babysit Effie five days a week, who is almost as old as Effie, and who they've told Effie is someone she used to know from the PTA, makes her oatmeal or pours her corn flakes. But Flora is off today because she has a podiatrist appointment.

In her old life, Effie would wake at five, have wheat toast with margarine, followed by coffee with a splash of skim milk. Then she'd wash the kitchen floor on her hands and knees and after it was dry, she'd wake Maeve and Stewart. Tom would come down when he was ready, after his shower, smelling of too much Old Spice. She did this every day except Sunday when she still woke at five, but on Sundays she put a chicken in the oven and went to church.

Maeve leans in to kiss her mother, and that's when the acrid smell of cleaning products becomes much more concentrated. "Did you clean the kitchen, Ma?" She says this knowing she didn't because she can see the flecks of silly string she and Peter missed when cleaning up Paige's Halloween party.

Effie scrapes up the last of her waffles and when she opens her mouth, Maeve realizes where the smell is coming from. She needs to sit down, but she manages to keep standing. "Show me what you ate, Ma."

Effie sets down her fork and licks her fingers. Like a game-show hostess, she shows Maeve the box of waffles in the freezer.

"And the syrup?" Maeve asks, although she already knows it isn't syrup her mother ate.

Effie opens the cabinet below the sink. "I don't know why you keep the syrup down here." She hands Maeve a bottle of "New and Improved Ajax with Ammonia." "I almost couldn't find it."

Maeve thinks she might throw up. She takes a steadying breath, opens the cabinet where they keep the actual Country Time syrup, and hands the bottle to her mother. "Is this what you were looking for?"

Effie says, "Did you want me to make you some breakfast, honey?"

"I need to make a phone call," Maeve says. She's shaking so hard her teeth rattle. "Stay here. Don't eat anything else." As if her mother will not forget these instructions as soon as Maeve leaves the room. She takes the Ajax with her into the bathroom, and, sitting on the edge of the tub, dials Poison Control.

The lady at Poison Control tells Maeve to have her mother drink a glass of milk. She tells her not to let her throw up. "It'll burn her all the way back up." She says this without a trace of panic. She says this as if she's telling her the handling fee is three dollars and fifty cents.

Maeve leans into the tub and dry heaves.

She calls her father, but it goes straight to voicemail. He never checks his messages, so she hangs up. Maeve isn't sure what she wants from him, except that she wants him to know there's a crisis here, too.

In the kitchen, her mother has clumsily dealt herself a game of solitaire. She's singing the chickadee song. Maeve pours her a glass of milk. "Can I have coffee?" Effie asks.

"Start with this," Maeve says.

While her mother takes small sips, Maeve texts Dr. B and says she isn't feeling well. He texts back to let him know if she needs anything and Maeve starts to cry.

All day she trails her mother, and all day her mother doesn't throw up. When Effie goes into the living room to watch "The Price is Right," Maeve rearranges the cleaning products from under the sink to the cabinet above the fridge. She stands on a chair to get up there. Then she paces from room to room, rearranging where she keeps the air freshener, the shampoo, the razor blades. She tries to see everything the way her mother would see it, the way she used to worry about the world when Paige was a toddler—as a curiosity, an invitation.

She calls her brother. "How could she not tell it tasted bad?"

Stewart says, "She's all right, though?" In the background, Maeve thinks she can hear waves. Is he at the beach?

Maeve says, "Have you heard from Dad?"

"You sure she doesn't need to go to the hospital?"

"I feel like Ma's getting worse, Stew. Just since she came to stay with me." Maeve can feel her throat closing in on tears.

Stewart says, "This isn't your fault. She was getting worse anyway."

"I bought the Ajax. I put it under the sink. I didn't wake up when she was making waffles."

"Frozen waffles."

"I should have heard her in the kitchen."

"I can try to come home sooner than Christmas." A seagull screeches from Stewart's end of the line.

"It's okay," she says. "I'm okay."

5

Maeve is ten and Anita Haverland has invited her over to help her decorate their Christmas tree. The Haverlands do not have children, although Maeve has been given strict instructions by her mother not to ask Mrs. Haverland about this. Until her mother tells her about the invitation to decorate the tree and the Haverlands' lack of children, Maeve had not given any thought to the idea that there could be adults who didn't have children. She supposes she might have realized the Haverlands didn't have children because she had never met any of their children, even though she's been out to dinner with her parents and the Haverlands at least three times and has even been to the Haverlands' house for dinner twice. Maeve assumed they had older children who didn't live with them anymore. She feels both confused by what Mrs. Haverland does with her time without children, and also excited by the idea that if childlessness is a possibility, there might be other things in life she hasn't considered.

The Haverlands' house is bigger than the one Maeve lives in with her parents and Stewart. It has an extra floor which the Haverlands' call their "game room" and which contains Ms. Pacman, an actual real arcade game. They also have a bump-out room they call the "sunroom." Maeve particularly likes the sunroom because it has windows on three sides and a big built-in window seat. She hasn't ever sat there, but she imagines curling up with a Nancy Drew and reading for an entire afternoon.

Maeve has never been in the Haverlands' living room. When she and her parents and Stewart have come for dinner, they've started off in the kitchen and then moved into the dining room. While the adults have drinks on the porch after dinner, she and Stewart have been allowed to watch TV in the den. The living room is not the den, although Maeve assumed it was until, on this tree-decorating afternoon, Anita Haverland ushered her into a room with a ceiling so high Maeve would not be able to touch it even on a trampoline.

The room is entirely white—the walls so shiny Maeve can see a shadowy reflection of herself, the carpet a soft downy white, two white leather couches, a white marble fireplace, fancy white chairs that look made for a queen. There are huge paintings framed in gold—white flowers and white trees and white fruit. Immediately, her favorite is the three-dimensional white leopard that hangs over the fireplace. There are white vases on clear tables, white reindeer on the mantle, an ivory statue as big as Maeve of a woman carrying a jug on her head. Most impressive of all is the chandelier dripping with crystals that are not white on their own, but reflect the white of the world around them.

Anita tells Maeve to throw her coat "anywhere." Maeve folds her shiny purple parka into as neat a rectangle as she can manage and places it over the back of the couch. She hopes she hasn't brushed against anything dirty today.

The house is very quiet, so Maeve guesses that Charlie Haverland, who has always reminded her of as the Green Giant guy even though Charlie isn't green and he wears a suit and not an outfit made of leaves, is working and not in some other room watching the end of the news and about to join them. She doesn't ask.

On an easel is a photograph of something white and incredibly shiny. "Can you tell what it's a picture of?" Anita asks when she sees Maeve looking at it.

Maeve shakes her head and bends forward so that her face is very close to the picture. She can see variations in the color, but she can't make out a single object.

Anita touches Maeve's shoulder and Maeve jerks upright. "I'm sorry," Maeve says.

Anita smiles and squeezes Maeve's shoulder. "Don't be sorry. I'll give you a hint. I take pictures of things that are their color."

Maeve thinks about this and looks at the picture, but she still doesn't know. She feels stupid and figures Anita Haverland will soon give up and just tell her.

"One example is celery. Have you heard of celery green? I have a photograph of that hanging in the kitchen." When Maeve still doesn't hazard a guess, Anita says, "Think of something a fancy lady might have a necklace made of."

Maeve looks at the picture again, and then smiles as it comes to her. "Pearl!"

Anita Haverland flings an arm around Maeve's shoulders and pulls her in for a hug. "Smart girl."

Maeve is certain no one has ever used that phrase to describe her before, at least not in the tone of delight Anita has just used. Her mother has said things like "You're a smart enough girl to know you should take your muddy shoes off before traipsing all over the house." Things that imply she's both smart and not all at once.

Anita smiles her toothpaste-smile. "Your father said you might be willing to help me decorate my tree and I'm so glad you agreed."

Maeve feels heat in her cheeks. She isn't sure why she's been asked, but she's very glad to be here.

"My niece usually helps me, but she and her parents are in Paris for a month. Can you imagine?" Anita makes her eyes wide and Maeve mimics the gesture back because she isn't sure what else to do. She really can't imagine Paris. She's read books with Paris in them, *Madeline* springs to mind, but she can't actually picture staying in a city so far away for a long time. Would they bring their tree on the plane or would they buy one there? What about all the decorations?

The tree is positioned next to the white piano. "It's a baby grand," Anita Haverland says. Maeve knows she's referring to the piano and she wants very badly to touch it but she thinks about the grease that's likely on her fingers from the peanut butter cookie Anita Haverland gave her when she walked in the door and so she keeps her hands at her sides.

The tree is very big and very full. The Haverlands have wrapped it in hundreds and hundreds of white lights which are already plugged in and sparkling so much Maeve almost doesn't want to ruin it with ornaments. Surely, Charlie Haverland helped with the lights. He must be like her father and figure that decorating is woman's work.

Anita Haverland offers Maeve a mug of Swiss Miss with mini marshmallows while they work and Maeve looks at the white rug. "Don't worry about that," Anita Haverland says. "Everything can be cleaned."

Maeve doubts very much that any amount of scrubbing would get a hot chocolate stain all the way out of this snow-white rug, so she shakes her head.

"Maybe when we're done," Anita says.

Anita hands Maeve the first box and Maeve opens it to find ornaments as big as baseballs, but smooth and shiny. Years later, Maeve will remember the cool heft of those ornaments between her palms, like something she didn't realize she'd always wanted.

There are delicate white reindeer made of glass, glittery snowflakes, and tiny paper flowers, all of which Maeve hangs with exquisite care. Anita Haverland presses a button on a remote control and Christmas music comes out of speakers in the ceiling. Maeve doesn't think she's ever been this happy in all her life. There's a small part of her that hopes the niece stays in Paris forever and that Maeve can be the one to help decorate the tree year after wonderful year.

The final box is the tree topper. Maeve expects an angel, because an angel would be just right, but Anita Haverland takes out a dove, soft and feathery and lighter than Maeve expected. Anita climbs up on the stepladder she's dragged out from the pantry. She tells Maeve to "spot her" and so Maeve stands with her hands tightly on either side of the ladder in case Anita Haverland slips. From this angle, Maeve can see the weave on her beautiful gray tights. She wants very badly to run a fingertip over those tights, just for a second.

"Ta da!" Anita says when the dove is secure. The dove is more perfect than any angel would have been. Maeve stares at it for so long her neck hurts.

"Here," Anita Haverland says. She stretches out on the carpet just under the tree and Maeve follows suit. It's dusk now, and the room is dim despite all the white. On her back with the tree glowing above her and the soft white carpet cushioning her, Maeve feels flooded with love.

In the kitchen, they have hot chocolate and two more

peanut butter cookies each and then Maeve's mother comes to get her. She stands at the door and says she can't stay for coffee even though Anita Haverland practically begs her to come in for just a minute. "At least see the tree," she says.

"I have a roast in the oven," Effie says in the tone of voice that leaves no room for discussion.

Maeve feels a tug of confusion. It's like she's done something wrong just by being here, but her mother said she could come.

In the car, Effie asks how it was and Maeve says it was nice.

Effie says, "It was your father's idea. Anita loves kids, he said. Anita misses her niece." Effie's voice is all sharp edges. "He said I should treat her like a babysitter, go get my hair done." Effie makes a noise that's something like a strangled laugh.

Maeve isn't sure what to say, so she says nothing.

"You have glitter all over your face," Effie says after a while.

Maeve looks at her hands and sees the sparkle. She thinks that Anita Haverland's beautiful carpet must be covered in glitter, too. She thinks that Anita Haverland won't mind her carpet being covered in glitter, that she might even take a picture of it.

"Why are you smiling?" Effie asks.

"I'm not," Maeve says.

6

The yellow of the therapist's office is more bile than butter, which will be Maeve's excuse not to come back. She's here because Dr. B caught her crying in the chart room. When he asked if she was all right, Maeve told him vaguely about her mother's worsening confusion, and how she's moved her mother into her guest room, and how, even though it's supposed to be temporary, she isn't sure it really will be.

When she called her father last night, she'd asked him straight out when he thought he'd be home. She didn't say she felt like taffy stretched to its limit. After a pause, he said, "I know it's asking a lot, but can your mother stay with you a while longer? Anita isn't out of the woods yet."

It was his gentleness that disarmed her. Always, when he asked her for things—to buy her mother a birthday present, to take out the trash, to help clear the table—he'd demanded it and Maeve had acquiesced because she felt like she had no choice. She didn't exactly feel like she had a choice now, but at least she felt like they were two adults having a conversation.

She wondered if it was his guilt that was softening him. *Had* he pushed Anita? She could imagine him angry, and with the coil of violence, but she couldn't see him pushing her and then acting like he hadn't. But then, he'd acted like a man not having an affair for most of Maeve's life. Maybe the fall had been an accident. Maybe he'd reached for Anita and she'd stumbled. Maeve could understand why he'd want to be there when she woke up but she couldn't take care of Effie by herself indefinitely.

And, god, Anita. A head injury was bad and Anita wasn't young. But she'd always been strong.

Dr. B led Maeve to the room they used for X-rays and sat her in the reclining chair and she wished he'd put the lead bib on her because she would have liked the weight of a heavy thing on her.

Dr. B is foreign, from one of the Slavic countries although Maeve can never remember which one, the B standing for something long and hard to say. She should know it by now, and the not-knowing makes her shy and reserved around him.

Maeve has worked for this dental office for eight years, part-time, and she's never fallen apart like this. But Dr. B is so nice that, in some ways, Maeve wishes she'd needed him sooner.

Dr. B suggested a therapist—a woman who is a friend of his wife's—and Maeve obediently took the first appointment on Monday after five.

Now she's here, in the spotlight of a parking lot lamp, on a floral couch with puss-colored walls pressing in on her. The therapist, Wendy, isn't even bothering to take notes, as if Maeve's problems are interesting only to Maeve. Wendy runs a French-tipped nail over a wreath brooch, and Maeve wonders if the brooch was a gift from Dr. B's wife. She imagines them exchanging tiny silver-wrapped packages over tea and cranberry mini muffins at a hotel by the ocean.

It's not even Thanksgiving, which is technically too soon for wreath brooches.

Maeve says she isn't feeling suicidal now, but if, say, a train barreled through the building right then, she might not get out of the way. Mostly because she's too tired. She knows what suicidal feels like. Wendy perked up when Maeve mentioned she tried to kill herself when she was a teenager. "Weakly," she said, but Wendy heard it as "weekly" and leaned way in. "Fifty-two times in a year is a strong cry for help," she said.

Maeve should correct her, should explain she only tried to kill herself once with a handful of acetaminophen and that she hadn't even locked the bathroom door. That by "weakly" she meant "not a serious attempt" and not "once every seven days." But, she's forty-five minutes into her hour and her father is home with her mother because Peter has his bowling league, Paige is at Becca's, and Flora, who showed up this morning in the exact same house dress Maeve had just bought Effie, had to be home for the plumber.

Dr. B told Maeve she needs to put herself first, which Maeve thought was the sweetest thing anyone said to her in a really long time, and also possibly the most misguided. He brought her a large iced coffee with cream from Dunkin Donuts which she sipped on throughout the day even though she felt jangly from the caffeine and bloated from the enormous amount of dairy. Yesterday, Maeve found her mother holding a conversation with the large rubber tree plant Maeve had in the corner of the dining room.

Maeve promised to take Paige driving tonight and Peter will be home from his bowling league by eight and Maeve thought they could have a late dinner together, or at least a quick drink. She did not offer sex because she knew if she fully reclined, she'd fall asleep and any version of standing up sex would take more energy than she has. She didn't even brush her teeth this morning.

Wendy stands and suggests Thursday and Maeve agrees

even though Thursdays are Peter's night to volunteer at the homeless shelter, and, with Thanksgiving only three weeks away, Maeve has yet to buy a turkey, a potato, or even a box of stuffing. She suggested to Peter that they make reservations somewhere that has a buffet and he puffed up like he was about to start singing "Tradition" like Tevye from "Fiddler on the Roof." "Nevermind," she said. "I'll figure it out."

He said he'd help her, and he would, but he wouldn't know what to buy if she sent him shopping, unless she gave him a very detailed list, and if she did that, she might as well just do the shopping herself.

On the drive home, Maeve thinks about her teenage self in her parents' pink bathroom with a handful of acetaminophen in her mouth. She stood in front of the mirror while she swallowed, but now she can't picture her face. She can only imagine Paige's, and that makes her drive faster, and then remind herself to be careful.

*****

Her father is pacing when she gets home. "The hospital called," he says before Maeve has even taken off her coat. "Anita opened her eyes."

Maeve feels a wash of relief and also relief at his relief. If he'd pushed her, he'd be nervous she'd tell. He wouldn't be happy to have her awake. Unless he thinks she won't remember. "That's great, Dad."

He's halfway down the walkway when he turns. "It's too soon to know much, but it's something." He smiles, which is such a rare thing that Maeve smiles back with genuine happiness.

In the kitchen, Effie frowns over a cup of hot chocolate

Tom must have made her. It hasn't been fully stirred, and bits of powder float on top. Effie says, "He sure was in a hurry."

Maeve takes a spoon and stirs her mother's hot chocolate. She can feel it's cool and she wonders if it's been sitting in front of Effie for a while or if Tom made it that way deliberately so she wouldn't burn herself. He could have at least stirred it better.

Maeve sets the spoon aside. She takes a deep breath. If she's going to ask, she needs to ask. What's the worst that can happen? "Do you remember what happened with Anita, Mom? On Halloween?" Deep down, she knows nothing good can come from this conversation.

"Anita! Why are we talking about her?" Effie pushes her mug away. "Are you trying to poison me?"

"Of course not, Ma." Maeve is sure there's no point in asking anything more, but she can't help herself. "I'm just wondering if you remember how Anita fell."

Effie glances around the kitchen, then lowers her voice. "Is she here?"

"No, Ma, she's not here. Was she coming up the stairs? Or going down to get something?"

Effie looks over her shoulder. "She's everywhere."

"What do you mean?"

Effie scowls. "Don't you see her?" She gets up and yanks the living room curtains closed.

"She's in the hospital, Ma."

"Who is?"

Maeve sighs.

"Don't give me that," Effie says. Her face has turned scarlet with anger or annoyance.

"Sorry," Maeve says. "Are you done with your hot chocolate?

I can help you to bed."

Later, when Maeve calls Stewart and tells him how Effie seemed to think Anita was everywhere, he says, "I never understood why you couldn't give that woman up. Especially when you saw what it was doing to Mom."

"Jesus, Stew. I was a kid. And Anita was my idol. Plus I didn't know about the affair."

"Not at first you didn't."

Maeve rubs cold cream into her neck with so much force it feels like strangulation. "And as soon as I found out—as soon as I knew—I ended the friendship."

Stewart's quiet for a minute and Maeve can hear the tinkle of windchimes and some soft harp music. He's probably fucking meditating. Finally, he says, "You ended it when Dad got fired. But you knew about it before that."

"I didn't know."

He's quiet again. "Maeve—"

"Maybe you knew, Stewart. But I did *not* know."

"Okay," he says. "Okay." And then, "Are you going to be alright?"

She takes a breath and feels it pinch in the flat spot between her breasts. "I'm fine."

"How was therapy?"

Maeve laughs. "It was weird."

"You'll get used to it." She can hear the smile in his voice. "I love you, kid."

"You, too."

7

Maeve is twelve and she's wearing pantyhose that have slipped down low enough to create a kind of hammock beneath the skirt of her dress and her underpants. Between that and her new heels, which are only an inch high but which she cannot seem to balance on without hunching over, she feels the opposite of elegant. Her mother told her she wouldn't like pantyhose or heels and so Maeve keeps her shoulders back and doesn't look down at the trouble that is her lower half.

Anita Haverland is having a showing of her photographs that are close-ups of things that are their color. It's being held in a gallery in Portland and Maeve has never been to a gallery anywhere and has only ever been to Portland for lunch.

"Do you need something?" Her mother said the last time Maeve suggested an afternoon of shopping in the Old Port.

Maeve said she just wanted to look and her mother said they'd go some day when the weather was nicer. "Most of the stores are dog-friendly," Effie said. Her mother preferred places that allowed her to bring Clipper, whom she's bought a wardrobe of jackets for.

And so, as her father drives overly cautiously through the narrow streets, Maeve tries to see as much as possible—the shop windows sprayed with aerosol snow, huge red ornaments dangling on silver chains, blue and green and red spheres hanging festively from lamp posts, party dresses and fur-trimmed wedding dresses on mannequins.

Finally, they pull into a parking garage and Maeve's mother makes a tsking noise and her father whacks the steering wheel with his palm and asks if she has a better idea and Effie says it's going to be expensive, that's all.

The sidewalks are brick and slippery and Maeve wishes her father would offer her an arm, but she's only ever seen that done in the movies. She's not moving fast, anyway, because she can barely pick up her feet with her pantyhose slipped so low.

Stewart has stayed home because he's fourteen and not interested in anything except Dungeons and Dragons.

The gallery is very warm and bright and Anita Haverland is wearing a green velvet dress that goes all the way to the floor, but when she turns to explain something about a photograph that Maeve thinks might be sand, Maeve sees that her back is entirely exposed. She's never seen a dress like that—a dress that is so completely one thing from the front and another from the back. Something that is modest and then not modest. Maeve sucks in her stomach.

Effie takes Maeve's hand. It's clammy and damp, but Maeve holds on anyway. "Oh," Effie says. "Oh." Maeve isn't sure if she's awed by the photographs, Anita's dress, or both.

Effie's dress is silky black with big pink roses. It came with a belt, but she'd decided it made her look "hippy" and so she left it on the bed. The empty hoops of the dress look much worse now than they did at home.

Along a wall festooned with paper lanterns is a long table with skinny glasses of champagne, tiny quiche, and some kind of miniature pancake. Maeve has been allowed a sip of wine or champagne from time to time, but never a whole glass. Her parents are across the room, standing side by side at the photograph of what Maeve guesses is grass. She takes the champagne and sips it, letting the bubbles pop on her tongue. There's a gap between her parents, wide enough for a person. And then Anita Haverland floats across the room and fills the space between them. She places a hand on each of their backs and Maeve sees her mother pull away while her father turns to face Anita. He is smiling, smiling, smiling. He has a nice, straight nose, and a firm chin. His eyes are the gray-blue of a New England ocean. Maeve has her mother's muddy hazel eyes. Her father laughs and nods and points and Maeve almost can't stand to see him this agreeable.

Her mother has hooked her thumbs through the loops of her dress and is smiling her cracked-face smile. Maeve wishes she'd told her mother to bring the belt, just in case.

Maeve finishes her champagne and eats two quiche in quick succession in order to quell the fuzziness of her stomach.

Her mother crosses the room, leans into Maeve's ear and says, "Don't make a pig of yourself."

"Did you try these?" Maeve offers her a quiche, but Effie pushes it away.

"Too much cheese."

Her mother loves cheese, although it's decidedly a "treat" food, and Maeve almost says so, but she catches her mother looking hard at the muscles lining Anita Haverland's bare back.

Maeve deposits the champagne glass behind the quiche. She wipes her mouth and most of her careful pale-pink lipstick comes off on the square gold napkin.

Her mother sips a glass of champagne. She says, "I wouldn't want any of these hanging in my house." She gestures to a picture of a peach and a bit of champagne sloshes out of the glass.

Maeve doesn't say how much more she likes these pictures

over the print of apples falling out of a basket which her mother has recently purchased from the Harriet Carter catalogue and hung in the kitchen, above Clipper's bowl.

Maeve particularly likes Anita's photograph of the skin of an orange. Looking at it, she can feel the bitter tingle on her tongue.

Charlie Haverland appears just then and wraps his arm around his wife's bare back. He shakes Maeve's father's hand with his other hand, making a kind of triangle with Anita Haverland and her backless dress in the center.

Charlie Haverland wears a pale blue suit with a bright red tie. Charlie has a long body and big hands and feet that make him look clownish, like he should be funny, except Maeve has never heard him say anything amusing. She can't remember if she's ever even seen him laugh. In that way, he's like Effie. Anita and Tom are the balloons, Effie and Charlie are the smooth stones anchoring the balloons to the table.

Her father doesn't like champagne and so Maeve thought he might not drink tonight, but she sees now that Charlie has brought him a bottle of Captain Morgan's and a two liter of Coke. He's pulled out a mug from the jacket of his suit, like a magic trick, and Maeve's father is as delighted as if he's just seen a rabbit pulled out of a hat.

Maybe Effie sees the mug, too, but now she's turned away to get closer to a picture Maeve guesses is a bowl of cranberries. Tonight, Effie wears her hair in a deep side part, held back on one side with three bobby pins and curled into a great puff on the other side. At home, Maeve told her it looked nice, and it did, but here it looks childish.

Maeve feels weightless and brave from the champagne. "Your hair looks really nice, Ma," Maeve says. She's trying to make up for letting her leave the house like that by lying more, and better.

Effie slings an arm around Maeve, pulls her into a side-hug.

When Anita Haverland appears beside Maeve and hands her a glass of juice, Effie releases Maeve from the hug and runs her fingertips over her hair. Maeve can tell it's juice because there are no bubbles and it's the yellow of apple juice, but she appreciates that Anita has put it in a tall skinny glass.

"Effie," Anita says, air-kissing the space next to Effie's cheek.

Effie smiles the smile she uses on cashiers who ring in the wrong price at the checkout. "You must be pleased with the turnout," Effie says.

Maeve can hear the displeasure in her mother's voice and she's positive Anita can hear it, too, but Anita just smiles wider, all the whiteness of her teeth like a fence around a bad dog.

Maeve wonders why her mother can't say a single nice thing about even one of Anita's photographs. Maeve says, "You said you thought the one of celery was interesting, didn't you, Ma?"

Effie blinks at her. "If you say I did, I must have."

Anita winks at Maeve. "They aren't for everyone. Don't give your Mom a hard time."

Effie stares at Anita for a moment, then blinks.

Anita says, "Maeve has been such a big help."

Effie tosses her head back and laughs. "And I always appreciate the free babysitting."

It's not a soft, real, or otherwise nice laugh. It's a laugh like a rash. Both Maeve and Anita inch back from Effie and, even though Maeve can feel Anita looking at her, she doesn't look back for fear she might cry.

When Effie excuses herself to the ladies' room, Anita leans in and kisses Maeve's cheek. "You look so pretty," she says.

Anita Haverland smells like oranges and her lips are cool and soft.

Maeve allows the compliment to rush over her. She tells Anita she loves her dress and Anita twirls, which causes many of the men in the room, including Maeve's father, to turn and watch her.

Maeve wants to say something smart about the photographs, but all she can think to ask is if Anita has a favorite. Anita says she loves them all for different reasons and Maeve can't think of anything to say after that and so she just stands there, nodding.

And then a man takes Anita's elbow and says something about purchasing and Anita smiles over her shoulder at Maeve as she glides away. Maeve's pantyhose feel dangerously low and she looks for a bathroom just as her mother reappears beside her. "Where's your father?"

Maeve hasn't seen him in the last few minutes, but she hasn't been looking, either.

And then Maeve sees him in the far corner of the room, his face a drunken pink, his finger on Charlie Haverland's chest. Maeve turns away before her mother can follow her gaze.

When her mother finally finds her father, she's all smiles and hands on his back and adjusting his collar.

Later, as they walk back to the parking garage, her father says, "Those pictures were really something."

Her mother's mouth creases downward, but she manages to nod.

"They're kind of weird," Maeve says.

Her father stops and looks at her. Maeve thinks he might

hit her, although he's only ever raised his hand, has never actually struck her. Still, she ducks.

He spits, not at her but near her, and then he turns and walks fast and Effie hurries after him and Maeve shuffles along behind them, pantyhose hammocking more and more.

8

Maeve barely closes the door behind her when her father is in front of her. He says, "Your mother ate peas and corn for dinner."

"Weren't there leftovers?"

He can't seem to get his left arm in his left NASCAR jacket hole and Maeve just watches him struggle, wondering if he's already too drunk to drive. This should worry her more than it does. She should offer to drive him to the hospital so that he doesn't get into an accident. Wendy-in-her-head nods encouragingly but Maeve doesn't have the energy to worry about anyone other than her mother. Her father will wear this jacket all winter, even though it isn't warm enough for winter.

He says, "She said she doesn't eat meat."

"Since when?" Maybe there are enough nutrients in the peas and corn. No protein, but definitely vitamins. C? A?

"How should I know?" Arm finally encased, he zips up.

Her father smells like Old Spice, which might be hiding the smell of rum, but Maeve doesn't call him on it.

"Were you able to give her a shower?" Maeve hates the way this sounds like she's talking about a dog, like Clipper, whom they'd had to bribe into the tub with pieces of roast beef.

Her father looks at the mud-streaked floor, at the dust on the ceiling fan, at the cluster of ladybugs who have escaped from the cold into the upper right-hand corner of the living room window. "She wouldn't let me," he says.

"Did you explain it to her? Did you remind her who you are?" Since Effie moved in, Maeve has joined an online Alzheimer's support group. Her mother doesn't have Alzheimer's, but she's had a series of small strokes that have a similarly damaging end result.

He clenches his teeth. "I shouldn't have to remind her."

Maeve is about to argue that none of this is fair to any of them, but her father holds up his hands. Like he might push her, although he's done that only once when she was fourteen and she told him she hated everything about him. "Don't," Maeve says, and he looks wounded.

"She's awake," he says.

Maeve blinks at him. "Is she watching TV?"

"Anita. The hospital called."

"Oh my god. That's great, that's wonderful." Maeve feels relief so palpable it's like someone has draped her in a silk robe. Anita will wake up and tell the nurses she fell and Maeve will go back to not trusting her father for all the usual reasons, not because she thinks he violently pushed the woman he's been having an affair with for more than three decades.

Tom's lips twitch into a half-smile. "She's not out of the woods yet."

Such a funny expression, Maeve thinks. She imagines Anita in her backless green dress emerging from a sound set of trees, music crescendoing.

"You must be so relieved," Maeve says.

He lifts his baseball hat and rubs his head. "Yeah. It was scary there for a while."

He doesn't look guilty, or afraid of what Maeve means by "relieved." Maeve thinks of the Haverland Health presentations he and Charlie Haverland used to give, how convincing they were. Is her father just a good actor?

They stand there, quietly for a few seconds. And then, before she can think better of it, Maeve asks, "What happened? The night she fell?"

Tom rubs his head again. "She fell down the stairs. It all happened pretty fast."

Maeve thinks of all the times he told Effie he wasn't at Anita's and how, even when Maeve had seen him there with her own eyes, she almost believed him.

Maeve lowers her voice. "Ma says you two were arguing and that Anita stepped back to get away from you and that's why she fell." Maeve doesn't say that she, Maeve, wonders if her mother is protecting Tom, if the truth is that he pushed Anita while they were arguing.

He pauses with the door open, a current of snow blowing in. "She told you that?"

If Maeve didn't know better, she'd think he looked hurt. "She told Paige and Paige told me."

He shakes his head. "You know your mother can't remember up from down these days." He doesn't sound worried or angry about what Maeve has just accused him of. Just defiant. Like always. "I'll call later," he says, and then he's just a cloud of Old Spice.

In the living room, her mother seems to have been swallowed by the couch. "You want ice cream, Ma?" Effie stares at the spot where they've always put the Christmas tree. She lifts her eyes to Maeve, shrugs.

"I'll set up the tree tonight," Maeve says. It's the first week of November, and what she really needs to do is give her mother a shower, but the Christmas tree seems like a thing that will cheer them both up.

Effie beams at her. "That sounds nice."

Maeve isn't sure if her mother means the ice cream or the tree, so she gets her a bowl of maple walnut and brings it in to her. Effie cradles the ice cream like it's a cup of tea.

"Do you want to help me put up the tree?" Maeve asks. She takes the spoon and holds it to her mother's lips.

"Oh!" Effie pushes back against the sofa cushions. "That's cold."

"It's ice cream." Maeve wipes the dribble off Effie's chin.

Effie hands Maeve the bowl. "Maybe you could heat this up?"

"How about some cheese and crackers?"

Effie closes her eyes. "I don't think so."

It's not like it will kill her mother to miss a meal. Last night, she ate macaroni and meatballs, garlic bread, and two slices of still-frozen chocolate cake. This morning, when Maeve came down from her shower, her mother was eating the rest of Peter's box of Shredded Wheat, which Maeve bought only two days ago. Her old mother said Shredded Wheat tasted like wet newspaper.

In the basement, Maeve unearths the tree box. She's aware of her mother alone upstairs, aware of her ability to turn on the stove and cover it with a blanket, or to walk outside thinking she heard someone and then forget why she's there or that she doesn't have shoes on. But she stands for a minute at the bottom of the stairs thinking about how easy it would have been for her father, even though he's not as big or strong as he once was, to push Anita. How angry he can be. How quickly she would have fallen. Does Anita remember what happened? Will she tell? Maeve imagines the police at her door, saying they have a warrant for Tom's arrest, taking him away in handcuffs. And Maeve feeling a tiny bit satisfied that he can't get away with everything.

She has her father's old desk lamp—green and brass—on a shelf above the washing machine. When he retired, she said she wanted it, but then she couldn't decide where to put it. Now, it's bent neck seems to Maeve a kind of rebuke.

Maeve walks backwards with the tree, tugging it, her back aching with every step. Sweating, she thumps the tree up the basement stairs and into the living room.

"What's that?" Her mother asks when Maeve finally drags herself and the box into the living room.

"I don't like the mess of a real tree." Maeve slides the yellow-tipped branches into the yellow slots, red into red, white into white, and so on.

Effie says, "Aren't you clever."

Maeve can't remember if her parents put up the tree last year or the year before. Three years ago was the last Christmas they had at the Ever-yellow, before Maeve offered to take it over. It was just easier, she said. It was time for her mother to take a break. Effie hadn't protested. Her former mother had hung garland above every door, wedged silver bows into potted plants, taped paper reindeer and handmade snowflakes in every window. Tacky Christmas, Maeve and Stewart called it. Maeve thought she'd be relieved to see it go away.

Maeve finishes wrapping the lights around the tree and hands her mother the box of ornaments. "Help me with these, Ma." And so, Effie holds out the blue clay star Maeve made in kindergarten, or the red bulb Paige painted at Camp Polywog, or the silver reindeer Maeve and Peter bought on a trip to Niagara Falls. With each ornament, Maeve chooses a branch and asks "Here?" Moving it down or to the left, "Or, here?"

Her mother holds out her hand for the reindeer and Maeve hands it to her, biting back a warning to be careful. Her mother runs her thumb along the wiry antler. "She was such a good baby."

"She was," Maeve says. Maeve's breath hitches in her chest. She doesn't know if her mother is thinking about Paige or about Maeve herself.

She waits for her mother to say more, but when she doesn't, Maeve unwraps the sleigh Stewart made from popsicle sticks. The red paint is streaky with age. She should send it to him, although she doubts Natalie does anything as traditional as putting up a tree. "Do you remember Stewart making this at camp? He wrapped it and gave it to you for Christmas when he was six." Maeve would have only been four, and she doesn't remember it, but she remembers her mother telling the story of it. The popsicle-sleigh was wrapped in the comic pages of the newspaper, tied with shoelaces Stewart had removed from his own sneakers.

Her mother gets quiet, and Maeve wonders if she's gone too far. Finally, Effie laughs. "He was a good baby, too.'"

Maeve smiles. She plugs in the tree and Effie claps. For a moment, they both quietly take in the glow of the lights. "What's your favorite Christmas carol, Mom?"

Effie thinks for a minute. "I like them all."

Maeve chooses to believe this. She chooses to believe her mother hasn't forgotten the names of all the Christmas carols.

Maeve starts to sing "Silent Night" because it's the first one she thinks of. She only knows the first verse, and so she begins and her mother joins in and they sing the first stanza over and over, until Maeve's mouth feels like sand and Effie falls asleep.

9

Maeve is twelve and so far, she finds sixth grade easier than fifth. When the teacher—a fat woman with a boy's haircut—asks the answer to a math problem, Maeve shoots her hand into the air and as soon as the teacher points, she starts to answer. But the teacher ignores Maeve and calls on the girl in front of Maeve, the girl who is both pretty and prettily named, with no hard sounds anywhere.

Maeve has been smiling and, even though she would like to stop, she keeps smiling so that the class will think she was just kidding around.

"Little Miss Know-it-all," the teacher sometimes calls her.

This time, the teacher says, "That's right, Lisa." She's all big-mouthed smile, which she never gives Maeve.

Maeve tells this to Anita Haverland. She has, in fact, waited to tell Anita. Maeve has not told her mother because her mother would tell her father and her father would say she needs to sit on her hands and give other kids a chance to answer. He'll add that she should "take it on the chin." He says that last one a lot, as if she and Stewart are boxers or he wants them to be.

Anita Haverland has asked her over to help her with her photography. This time, she's having Maeve sort out the greenest peas from a bowl of previously frozen peas. She has her roll them on a paper towel to blot their wetness but not smoosh them.

Anita says, "She sounds like a witch."

Effie encouraged Maeve to go to Anita's today because Effie is washing the walls with a solution of white vinegar and warm water and she doesn't want Maeve underfoot. When Anita called, Maeve offered to stay and help (she knows how to make the solution of one part vinegar to three parts water) but her mother said no, she should go have fun. The way she said was like she was telling Maeve to go have a tooth pulled, but Maeve put on her coat and boots and waited by the door for her mother to dry her hands and find her keys.

Anita praises the peas Maeve has selected, declaring them undoubtedly the best in the bunch and Maeve "very clever" and so Maeve figures this is the perfect time to tell her what Mrs. Phalen said about her being a know-it-all.

"Who lets this woman keep teaching?" Anita has stopped arranging the peas into a white bowl and looks at Maeve with all her might.

Maeve's eyes prick with tears of gratitude.

Anita returns to the business of sorting peas and after a few minutes, she says, "My guess is that she's jealous of you. Because you're the whole package."

Maeve smiles even as tears puddle and roll. She pictures herself tied up with a giant red bow. Her mother has told her not to let compliments go to her head. Finally, when her mouth feels like it will stay in place, Maeve says, "She's a grown-up, though."

"Probably stuck in a job she hates. Probably wishing she had her youth back and that she was even half as smart as you."

Being called smart is like eating rock candy. It fizzes her all over.

Anita drags a chair over to the counter so she can stand on

it and take the picture of the peas from above. Maeve thinks this is very clever. Anita kicks off her heels and climbs onto the chair in her stockings. They are the color of skin, but shiny and smooth, unlike her mother's which often look fuzzy in places, baggy in others. Anita asks her to hold the chair and Maeve holds tight. She wishes, though, that she could hold Anita Haverland's silky legs.

10

After one of the Autistic kids Peter works with pokes him in the eye with the eraser end of a pencil (accidentally, Peter says, as if Maeve would think something else, would accuse the kid of malicious intent), he starts wearing the eye patch Maeve wore on Halloween.

"Have you been to the eye doctor?" Maeve asks. It's the Saturday before Thanksgiving and Paige is home with Effie so they can get what they need without worrying she'll go outside and invite random people in for dinner. She did this once already, with the UPS guy, who seemed hungry and grateful to be asked in for dinner, but none of them really knew what to say to him. And Effie, because she immediately forgot he was there on her invite, kept telling him he looked familiar.

She's told her father this, told him her mother needs to get home, that being at Maeve's is only making her more confused. Maeve expected a fight, but her father just said he knew. He said things would go back to normal soon. He sounded exhausted, which made Maeve sorry she'd said anything.

Every time Maeve asks Peter to get something on the left side of the store, he swivels his entire body.

Peter says, "It feels fine as long as I don't try to look out of it."

Maeve tosses a box of stuffing into the cart and Peter picks it up. "I thought you hated boxed stuffing."

"I don't have time to hate boxed stuffing. Have you seen

the canned cranberry sauce? Did we go by it?"

Peter taps the eye patch. "I'll keep an eye out for it." He laughs and Maeve manages a half-smile in return. She misses the version of herself who laughed at everything he said.

Maeve pushes the cart hard down the next aisle, grabbing dried onions, Diet Coke, canned pumpkin pie filling, and pre-made crust. She won't feel guilty that she's not making from-scratch cranberry sauce or stuffing or pie, the way she always has. She's making the turkey and the potatoes and she's going to get her mother dressed and at the table with her teeth in and if anyone wants more from her, they can go to hell. Wendy-in-her-head asks Maeve why she's so angry and Maeve-in-her-head storms out of Wendy's office.

Why is there no cranberry sauce anywhere? Maeve stops at the instant mashed potatoes. It would be so much easier than peeling and boiling and draining and mashing, but she imagines the look of disdain on Paige's face and passes them by. She's over by the turkeys, deciding on how small she can go this year, when Peter catches up to her and slides an arm around her waist.

"Hey," he says. When she turns toward him, she sees he's commandeered a banana for a microphone, into which he mouths the words to "Nights in White Satin," which is playing over the grocery store's speakers.

And just like that, Maeve is crying.

Peter drops the banana into the cart. "Hey." He pulls her into his chest, into the no-longer-soft Rudolf sweater he's worn for so many years it's pilled and stretched. "We can eat out for Thanksgiving if that's easier?"

Maeve wipes her eyes and then her nose on her sleeve. Dignity be damned. "I loved Anita Haverland. My father loved her—which he shouldn't have—but I loved her, too. I shouldn't feel bad about loving her. I shouldn't feel bad for feeling bad that she's hurt."

"No one thinks you should feel bad, honey."

Maeve sniffs. "That's not true. My mother hated my friendship with Anita. She made me feel so shitty about it. But I didn't know they were having an affair and then when I knew—we weren't friends after everything came out. It was just—poof—over. But no one acted like I had any right to miss her or be upset. No one even talked to me about it. And now, she almost died. And my father—have they been having an affair all this time? They have—of course they have." Maeve gulps back more tears and ignores the woman in the Santa-patterned pajama pants staring at her. As if she's one to judge.

Peter says, "It's so complicated."

"They've been having an affair all these years. That's so messed up." What Maeve doesn't say is *and I gave her up.* "And why, if my father—" she lowers her voice, "—*pushed* her—why wouldn't she have told someone by now? Why is she letting him sit by her bedside like he's the good guy in all of this? Do you think she just doesn't remember?"

Peter strokes her hair. "Maybe we should go see her."

Maeve rolls her head side to side across his chest. "The last time I saw her I called her a homewrecker." She pulls away from his now-damp sweater.

Peter nods. "You were just a kid." He puts his arm around Maeve's waist like they're on the beach, arm in arm, and not in front of a full grocery cart in the canned goods isle, blocking people from the peas and corn.

*****

When they're backing out of their spot, Maeve regrets agreeing to go see Anita. "We should get the groceries home," she says.

But Peter's the one driving and he puts his hand on Maeve's knee and squeezes. He says, "I think this is important, honey. It'll feel cathartic to see her. You'll see that she doesn't hold what you said against you. And maybe she remembers how she fell. It was probably like your father said—she went to get something from the basement and it was just an accident. Think how much better you'll feel once you hear it from her."

"Or she could tell me to fuck off." Maeve digs through her purse in the hopes she's shoved a compact in there, but there's nothing, not even a packed down, mostly useless one.

"You didn't do anything wrong, Maeve. Your Dad had the affair."

"I loved Anita more than I loved my own mother." It's the first time she's said it aloud and the truth of it sets off a series of bombs in her intestines.

When they pull into the hospital parking lot, Maeve opens her door and vomits up her afternoon coffee.

Peter hands her a tissue. He's so ready with the tissues, it makes Maeve feel worse about herself.

"We should go home," Maeve says.

He rubs her back and waits until Maeve wipes her mouth one last time, crumples the tissue and sticks it into her pocket, and gets out of the car. She hopes they'll be stopped at the front desk and told Anita can't have visitors. Instead, the board receptionist points to a gallon-sized jug of hand sanitizer and asks who they're there to see. She tells them third floor, room 304.

Maeve says, "I hope the groceries will be okay in the car."

"It's twenty-five degrees out." Peter squeezes her hand.

A left off the elevator and they get to Anita's room in twelve steps. The first thing Maeve notices are the flowers. Two hospital pitchers, one white bud vase, two clear vases, and three plastic cups all have roses, carnations, daisies, and lilies in them. The room smells like perfume layered over disinfectant layered over old pee.

The second thing Maeve notices is her father. He's sitting by the window, half in shadow, his feet on Anita's bed, his head lolled to the side. He's sound asleep.

The third thing she notices is that Anita is sitting up and her eyes are open. Somehow, Maeve thought awake from a coma would still mean a tube down her throat. Maeve thought she'd say what she needed to say to someone only partially lucid, and then they'd get out of there.

"Maeve," Anita says. Her eyes are purple-shadowed, her skin nearly translucent. She's hooked up to monitors and bags emptying things into her body and taking things out, but she's alert.

Maeve can taste the remnants of vomit in her mouth.

Anita swallows. "I wasn't sure you'd come."

It's been thirty years since Maeve last saw Anita Haverland. She was wearing a wine-colored coat with a faux fur collar. Her blond hair was pinned back in a twist and, even though it was breezy on the deck of the Haverlands' house, not a single hair was out of place. When Maeve called her a homewrecker, Anita's eyes fluttered downward, but only for a second. When they came back to meet Maeve's, they were like chips of ice. She said, "You might see things differently someday. But I am truly sorry I hurt you, Maeve." It was on "truly" that she ripped the film from Maeve's camera.

Now, she's wearing a white hospital gown patterned with tiny blue flowers, half off one shoulder, but she looks as defiant as she did that day on the deck.

Tom blinks awake. "Oh, hey," he says.

A nurse glides in, all cheer, all smiles. "You can't all be in here at once," she says. "Just two at a time."

Maeve wants to be the one to leave, to not notice that her father has his shoes off and that he has a half a roll of Lifesavers on Anita's rolling table.

Peter says, "I can go grab us all some coffee."

Maeve holds onto his arm. "My husband," she tells Anita.

"Nice to meet you." Her smile seems sticky, like her mouth is dry.

A good, faithful man, Maeve wants to say.

Tom stands and reaches for the pink water pitcher next to Anita, holds it out to her, and guides the straw to her lips. When she finishes drinking, he says, "I need to visit the little boy's room anyway." He slips on his shoes.

When he's gone, Maeve says, "We can't stay long."

"I'm glad you came." Anita smiles and touches the oxygen tube under her nose. Maeve can't remember ever seeing her without lipstick. She looks like a pastel version of herself.

"How are you?" Maeve sits in the chair her father has just vacated, mostly to keep herself from collapsing. It's uncomfortably warm from him. Peter sits on the windowsill.

"I've been better," Anita says.

She's not surprised that Maeve has come, which makes Maeve feel a little pathetic. She's still the little girl who'll find a way to spend time with Anita even when she should be home with her own mother.

There's a sheet covering Anita to her waist. Her hospital

gown has slipped off her bony shoulders and Maeve reaches over and lifts one side and then the other. Anita leans forward. "Can you re-tie the back?"

Maeve leans closer. Under the hospital smell, there's still the faint smell of oranges. Or maybe Maeve is imagining it. Anita's skin is warm and damp and Maeve thinks of her on the beach, sunlight grabbing the backs of both of their necks, heat rising from the sand as Anita bent to photograph its grains. Maeve makes a bow with the two sides of string. "There," she says.

Peter pushes off from the window sill. "I'm going to get some coffee. How about you ladies?"

Anita shakes her head. "I'm okay," Maeve says. She knows he's just looking for a way to give them time to be alone and she wants to tell him to stay, but she can't do that without seeming even more like a child.

When he's gone, Anita asks after Paige. She says, "Tom says she's beautiful. And smart."

Maeve feels the gap of all the years without Anita open like a chasm before her. Paige is the same age Maeve was when she last saw Anita. It would take too many words to fill the space, so Maeve says nothing.

Anita says, "Your Dad says she's a big help with Effie."

Maeve flinches. "I'm not sure I want to talk about them."

Anita nods. "I'm sorry."

Maeve wants the apology to be for everything—for having an affair with Tom, for hurting Effie, for befriending Maeve when she had to know it would end badly, and for Effie sliding away now, which obviously Anita knows.

Maeve feels adrift and so she picks up the hairbrush from Anita's bedside table and Anita closes her eyes and nods. When

Effie allows it, Maeve has been curling her hair. Effie's hair is short now, a sensible cut to her ears, boyish, un-dyed and so the color of steel. Tom says she wanted it cut, but Maeve thinks it was his idea, because it's easier for him, and she can't really blame him for that. With the curling iron on low, Maeve makes a ridge of curls across the top, then musses them with her fingers so that her mother looks impish. Sometimes Effie smiles at her reflection and sometimes she looks perplexed by the old woman reflected back at her.

Maeve stands, unpins Anita's hair, which is more white than blonde, but still thick and shoulder-length. She starts at the ends and brushes up, untangling gently. From outside the room, there's the murmur of nurses and doctors going about their business, the beep of call bells and machines, the hum of TVs. Maeve hasn't been this close to Anita in more than two decades, but everything about her feels as familiar as it did at the height of their friendship, if that's what it was, when Anita would put her arms around Maeve and hold the camera to her eye and point and say, "See it? There?"

When Anita's hair is all smoothed out, Maeve brushes from the top down, slow and steady strokes. Anita sighs. "You're a good girl."

Maeve says, "Can you tell me what happened? How you fell?" Anita, she's sure, will tell her it was an accident. She'll explain about the paperwork she needed—maybe they're selling Haverland Health now that Charlie's sick—and how her ankle gave out and that she remembers trying to grab the railing, but it went right through her hands.

Anita opens her eyes and puts a hand on Maeve's hand, which is still holding the brush against Anita's hair. "I didn't fall."

Maeve's hand turns to stone. It's true, then. Anita and Tom were arguing and Tom pushed her. Maeve can see it all so clearly—the way his face reddens high on his cheeks when he's mad, the way he bites back on his teeth, the way his shoulders arrow toward his ears. She can see Anita's face change from laughter to worry to fear, the way it did that day he grabbed her arm and shook. She can see the step backwards, the heel just over the step's edge, the flail backwards. Maybe Tom reached for her, tried to stop the fall, but it was too late.

Maeve is about to ask how Anita can forgive Tom, how she can allow him to spend all this time at her bedside, alleviating his guilt, when Anita says, "I didn't fall. Your mother pushed me."

11

Maeve is thirteen and Stewart is fifteen and the Linden's are having a "holiday" lunch with Charlie and Anita Haverland at DiMillo's. It's still weeks before Christmas and only Maeve is singing Christmas carols on the hour-long drive to Portland. Effie says it might snow and Tom says if it does, they'll stay at a hotel and Effie asks when he became made of money. He doesn't say anything else and so Maeve hopes that means they really will get to stay in a hotel.

Maeve loves the idea of staying in a hotel, but only if she and Stewart can have their own room. She doesn't like the way her father smells at night—of unbaked bread and stomach acid—or the look of her mother's unclothed knees. DiMillo's is a boat that's been turned into a restaurant and Maeve was so charmed by the idea that she wore her white dress with the sunflowers along the hem, even though her mother said that was a summer dress and too fancy, anyway. Maeve wishes Effie would let her be.

Maeve likes the slight sway of the boat and the way the tables are all pushed up close to one another so you can hear the hum of other conversations. By the time the waiter fills their water glasses and her father interrupts him to ask for a Captain and Coke, Maeve is listening to the couple behind her talk about their daughter's upcoming wedding in which there will be twelve bridesmaids. They sound cheerful about the enormous cost and chaos of dresses and gifts and shoes.

Maeve imagines herself the bride, carrying a huge bouquet of sunflowers, walking with both her parents—which she saw in a movie and Effie said was so sweet—down an aisle of yellow petals tossed from her flower girl's basket which is shaped to look like a tidy nest.

Anita and Charlie Haverland arrive like celebrities— Anita wearing big sunglasses and Charlie waving at them as though they might not see him in his red silk shirt. Anita tells Maeve she looks lovely and Maeve says Anita does, too, because she does. She's wearing a tight leopard-print dress and Maeve has never seen anyone wear leopard-print and not look like they're doing a bad job of imitating Loni Anderson, who Maeve knows from reruns of *WKRP in Cincinnati*.

Her mother clicks her tongue when she opens the menu, and Maeve assumes her upset has to do with the prices and not the choices, because Maeve has never seen such a big menu. "What's 'Florentine'?" Maeve asks and Effie laughs and squeezes her knee under the table and Maeve takes this to mean that Effie doesn't know and Maeve has just embarrassed her.

When Effie excuses herself to "freshen up," she touches Maeve's shoulder in a way that Maeve understands means she's to follow. In the bathroom, which is still damp from cleaning and smells like the powdered cleanser Effie uses in the tub, Effie yanks open her purse and digs around for her lipstick, which Maeve can see is right on top. When Effie's fingers finally find the tube, she pulls it out, uncaps it, and reapplies a thick coat of Royal Red. She smacks her lips and then says, "Everything is expensive here. Don't order more than you can eat."

"Have you been here before?" Maeve asks.

Effie fluffs her hair with her fingers, then wets her hands and tries to tame her bangs into place. "I don't know how that woman can sit there in that dress and act like she's so much better than everyone else."

Maeve doesn't need to ask who her mother is talking about. "I think she looks nice," Maeve says before she can stop herself.

"You would," Effie says.

Maeve isn't sure what her mother means by that—that Maeve doesn't have good taste? That Maeve likes Anita no matter what?—but it stings, anyway. "Why can't I like her?"

Maeve tries to keep the tears in, but they spill out and her mother sighs and hands her a wad of toilet paper she's ripped off from the roll. "You can like her." But her voice says the opposite.

When Maeve composes herself and they return to the table, her father is laughing at something and her mother yanks out her chair and part of the tablecloth and everyone's water sloshes a little. Anita Haverland makes a joke about being on a boat and Maeve's father laughs harder, so that Maeve can see the fillings that take up both sides of his bottom teeth. Anita says, "Tom, you make me feel like the cleverest woman on earth."

Anita is all big-smile, but Effie is not smiling.

The waiter comes back and smiles like he, too, is in on the joke.

Stewart orders the chicken fingers and Maeve says she'll have the same even though the lobster pie sounds like something she'd like much, much better. It's three times as much money as the chicken fingers so there's really no question about what she should do.

Maeve eats two pieces of bread with a glob of the whipped butter that has flecks of green in it. When Maeve reaches for her third piece, Effie grabs her wrist so hard, Maeve yelps. "You'll spoil your supper," she says.

Their food comes and of course Effie has ordered a salad with dressing on the side and of course the salad comes with the dressing on it and Tom tells her to just eat it and she pushes it away and gives him one of her stormy looks. He drinks from a glass that is way too pale to have much Coke in it and cuts into his bloody steak and leans over to Anita and Charlie and says how Effie eats like a bird. Which might have been a compliment, or her mother might have seen it as a compliment in some other circumstance with some other people, especially if one of those people was not Anita Haverland, who was the kind of woman who men tracked with their eyes while their mouths twitched with interest.

Instead, Effie says, "You don't want me to get fat, do you?"

Stewart says, "Aw, Ma, you're not even in the same zip code as fat." Effie beams at him.

For dessert, Charlie gets an ice cream sundae which is as big as anything Maeve has ever seen, bigger even than the one Stewart made when their parents took them to the make-your-own sundae place on Old Orchard Beach. The one delivered to Charlie Haverland is bigger than his wife's head, which everyone in the whole of DiMillo's knows because Charlie holds the goblet up next to Anita's teased hair and everyone at nearby tables cranes their necks to see what's going on. Maeve's mother looks like she's swallowed an entire wheel of banana from the banana-whatever Tom ordered and which came out on fire. Effie had said no, she didn't want dessert, whether it came out flaming or not, but Tom insisted and now his dessert has become dull compared to what surely seemed like an innocent ice cream sundae.

Anita laughs with her head back and Maeve notices she has no fillings. Just miles and miles of white teeth and pink tongue and her breasts bobbing up and down as she laughs. Tom laughs, too, and Stewart and Charlie Haverland. Maeve picks off a piece of her brownie, which is delicious but which she resists saying anything about. She pushes her plate toward her mother. "Do you want a bite?"

Effie shakes her head. Maeve's brownie and the fudge from Charlie Haverland's sundae make the air smell like chocolate.

When the check comes, her father and Charlie Haverland both grab for it. Anita puts her hand on top of Tom's. Her diamond ring is as big as a nickel. She says, "Let us. You guys can get it next time." Her voice sounds like a cat's purr.

Effie excuses herself to the bathroom again and this time she doesn't ask Maeve to come with her. When she returns, her eyes are puffy and Maeve can smell the powder her mother uses on her cheeks and nose. Maeve hates that her mother hates the Haverlands, especially because they make Maeve feel so full of happiness.

12

Maeve wakes to the smell of onions frying in butter and, before she remembers that Effie isn't the same mother she used to be, Maeve thinks her mother has started the stuffing. But, no, it's Thanksgiving, and Maeve woke at seven this morning to get the twenty-pound turkey in its pan on a bed of onions, garlic, and carrots, and get the whole thing in the oven. It was too early to start anything else, and she hadn't slept well, so she went back to bed for an hour. Now, she squints at the clock and sees that it's nearly ten and then she's bolt upright because the turkey needs to be basted.

In the kitchen, she finds a boy with his front pressed to Paige's back, his arms locked around her middle as if he might perform the Heimlich. The boy has a mohawk, not a tall one, but a strip of stiff brown hair between two shaved edges.

Maeve waits a moment to see if a piece of toast hurtles out of Paige's esophagus, but when Paige laughs and nestles her head into Mohawk boy's chest, Maeve coughs. Paige looks at her. "Hi, Ma. Morning." Paige pretends to slice butter and Maeve supposes Mohawk boy is meant to be helping.

When did she get so easy with herself?

Paige doesn't move out from under Mohawk boy's embrace. "We were going to wake you, but Dad said you needed your sleep. We basted the turkey."

When did Paige learn about basting? What else does she know? Maeve opens the oven and the turkey looks lovely and glistening. She can feel Paige and Mohawk boy watching her.

Maeve wants to feel warm and open and friendly toward this boy who is showing great affection for her daughter, but what she feels instead is like she's been caught outside in a hail storm. Maeve closes the oven and smiles as wide and bright as a jewelry lady on QVC. "Turkey looks great." She sticks out her hand toward the boy. "I'm Paige's Mom."

He finally releases a hand from Paige's waist. "Kris," he says, all smiles and big teeth.

Maeve shakes it with the grip her father taught her, and she registers the surprise in Kris's eyes. She releases his hand and turns to Paige. "Where's Dad?"

"Food pantry."

Maeve nods. Every year, Peter and a bunch of other charitable people give out turkeys and bags full of stuffing, cranberry sauce, and potatoes. He's wonderful. She knows because everyone tells her.

"And your grandmother?"

"Napping."

Maeve doesn't need to ask about her father. He's at the hospital with Anita. He said he'd be over in time to eat, but that he didn't want to leave Anita alone all day. He slept at the Ever-yellow last night, as he has most nights, because he said Effie's restlessness keeps him awake. Or maybe he slept at the hospital. Maeve doesn't really know. She was tempted to drive by and check for his car at the house, but what would it prove if it wasn't there? He and Anita aren't having sex in her hospital bed, surely.

Your mother pushed me.

If Anita's claim is true, Tom would have seen it. Maybe he understands that this is all his fault—that if he hadn't carried on with Anita, none of this would have happened. Has he begged Anita not to call the police? Not to press charges? Has he said Effie is too fragile, too confused? Has he convinced her it was an accident? Or was Anita lying to Maeve? Is it a story she and Tom have concocted together—make Effie the aggressor, make Tom the innocent. Effie, who can't remember enough to come to her own defense, would be the perfect scapegoat.

When they finally unwrap themselves, Mohawk boy deposits pats of butter on top of the stuffing. "So it'll brown," he says, as if Maeve hasn't made stuffing for the twenty-five Thanksgivings of her adulthood.

There's a bloom of pimples along his chin.

Maeve wants to be grateful that her daughter is trying to be helpful, but even from across the kitchen, Paige smells like sex and coffee. Wendy-in-her-head asks her if this is true or if she's just imagining it.

"Are you staying for dinner, Kris?"

Paige glances up and Maeve, for just a second, sees the little girl she was not long ago. "Is that not okay?"

"Of course it's okay," Maeve says, feeling the stiffness of her smile, like a plaster cast of her face. "Won't your family miss you?"

Kris shakes his mohawked head. "They're all doing their own thing."

"Okay," Maeve says, clapping her hands like she might break into a cheer. "Turkey is coming along, stuffing is ready to go into the oven, who wants to start peeling potatoes?"

Stewart calls as Maeve is opening a can of cranberry sauce. "Happy turkey day!" He says, so brightly she wonders if he's high.

"Where's your grandmother?" Maeve asks Paige. Stewart will want to talk to Effie.

"Still asleep."

Maeve heads down the hall with the phone pressed to her ear, listening to Stewart talk about the squash casserole they made with tofu and almond milk. The bedroom is dark, and Maeve crosses the room to open the curtains instead of flipping on the overhead and startling her mother. Stewart is still talking, even though she told him to hang on. He's telling her they're having a Tofurky because he and Natalie are going vegetarian and considering veganism for "health and the welfare of the planet." Maeve is making noises of being impressed when she slams her foot into the dresser she could have sworn she was nowhere near.

"Goddammit."

"You okay?" Stewart interrupts his soliloquy about the benefits of a plant-based diet.

"Not really."

"Who's there?" Effie sounds frightened, which Maeve feels bad about.

"It's me, Mom." Maeve reaches the window and pulls back the curtain and when she turns to the bed, she sees Effie sitting on the bed, naked from the waist up but wearing pants, at least. She hands the phone to her mother. "It's Stewart."

"What's Stewart?"

"On the phone."

Maeve rummages in the drawer for a bra and by the time she finds one and brings it over to her mother, she's dropped the phone on the floor. Maeve gets her mother's arms into the straps and hooks the bra. "That's nice, dear," her mother says, admiring her cleavage.

Maeve smiles at her mother's genuine delight. "Stay put while I find you a blouse." She picks up the phone on her way to the closet, but Stewart is gone, back to his Tofurkey and organic green beans and fucking normal life.

By the time she gets her mother buttoned into a blouse and gets back downstairs, Paige and Kris have set the table, Peter is home, and Tom is just pulling into the driveway.

"We did all the mashed potatoes," Paige says. Maeve nearly starts to cry with gratitude. "Are you okay, Mom?"

Maeve nods and goes in to check the turkey. Paige and Kris follow. Paige says, "I was going to make the green bean casserole but I couldn't find the stuff for it."

The button on the turkey has popped. Maeve keeps staring into the oven as if the turkey might somehow produce the green beans, cream of mushroom soup, and fried onion rings that she did not buy. "No green bean casserole this year, honey," she says, more to the turkey than to Paige.

Her father comes in, stomping snow off his boots, rustling out of his jacket. Maeve hopes his arrival will be enough to distract Paige from the absence of green bean casserole.

Paige makes a little squeak. "It's my favorite, though."

Kris mimics her, "It's my favorite, though," and does an exaggerated pout. It's not funny, and it doesn't even seem like he means to be funny. Paige swats at him, all smiles, and he swats her back, not smiling.

"Hey," Maeve says.

Paige says, "We can go get the ingredients. We have time—I swear it will be like two minutes."

And then her mother is in the kitchen eating one stuffed mushroom and then another and then another and Tom says, "You're going to get a stomach ache," and Effie says, "Are you my father?" in a way that seems like a sincere question, which makes Tom huff and stomp off into the living room where he immediately turns the TV on full volume.

"Everything's ready, Paige. And there won't be any stores open."

Paige has Maeve's purse open and is rummaging around for her keys. "Cumby's is open."

"They aren't going to have the stuff for green bean casserole."

"They might." Paige holds up the keys, pleading. "Kris has his license."

Maeve looks at her fine, needy face. She can give her this one thing, and maybe it will erase all the things she hasn't gotten right lately. "Go. But don't be long."

They're gone in a flash of arms in coats, arms around waists, and feet shoved into shoes.

Peter comes in with two apple pies.

"I bought pie," Maeve says.

"Your mother ate them. I grabbed these from the pantry. We had plenty."

"Are you selling those?" Effie asks.

"She ate both?" Maeve asks.

Peter kisses Effie on the cheek. "Hi, Ma, it's me, Peter."

Effie blushes and giggles. "I know, dear."

Peter lifts the turkey out of the oven and sets it on the counter.

"I didn't know Paige had a boyfriend," Maeve says.

Peter takes out the big knife. "Yeah. Few weeks now. They seem serious."

He doesn't mean it as a dig, but Maeve feels the pinch of not being the kind of mother who pays attention anymore. "I guess so if he's coming to Thanksgiving dinner."

Peter seems unfazed by Maeve's irritation. "I only know because I saw them holding hands when I went to pick her up after work," he says. "Should I wait to carve until they get back?"

It's almost an hour before they return with cans of green beans, mushroom soup, and the fried onion rings. In that time, Maeve has acquiesced and given her mother a slice of pie, a cup of tea, and two scoops of mashed potatoes. They look rumpled and glowing. "Cumby's had everything?" Maeve asks. She opens and drains both cans of green beans. She should talk to Paige about sex, which she has, so far, only told her the scientific what and how of things and that was years ago, when Paige was a sweet, innocent child. Maeve had drawn a happy face on both the sperm and the egg.

"We had to go to Windham. We found the green beans at Cumby's but then had to go to Big Apple for the other stuff."

Or they had sex in the car behind the elementary school. Maeve doesn't want to think about it.

Maeve gets out the casserole dish while Paige opens the soup. Effie slides a pat of butter between an unheated roll. "How can you still be hungry, Ma?"

"You talk to her like she's a little kid," Paige says.

"You won't be the one up with her all night when she's getting sick."

"She's hungry."

"Maybe we shouldn't have made her wait while you went out for green bean casserole."

"Maybe you shouldn't have forgotten it to begin with."

"Jesus."

"Language," Effie says, mouth full of bread.

Once the green bean casserole is finally cooked, the turkey finally carved, and everything else has been set out on the table, Maeve calls her father in from a rerun of Bonanza. "When did you come in?" Effie asks. She seems delighted.

"Just now," Tom says, kissing her cheek, playing along for once. "You look nice."

You'd never know, looking at them, that they were anything but happy. Peter squeezes Maeve's hand and she squeezes back.

"Let's eat," Maeve says.

Effie reaches for mashed potatoes and when half the spoonful falls onto the table cloth, she scoops them with her fingers.

"Don't do that," Tom says, pushing her hand away from the potatoes.

Effie swats at him. "You leave me alone!" She shouts and little pieces of potato fly out of mouth.

Kris laughs, his full mouth of chewed food on display, if only for a second.

Tom rears back, hands raised in defense. The rest of them pause, forks raised. Maeve says, "Mom—"

"Don't you start with me, too," Effie says.

They all wait, suspended, until Effie starts to eat again as if nothing at all just happened.

*****

Later, Effie lays down for a nap and Peter, Paige, and Kris go for a walk. Maeve finds her father watching Hogan's Heroes.

"Don't you get tired of watching the same thing over and over again?"

He shrugs. "They're funny."

Maeve watches with him as Hogan flirts with his secretary. "Wasn't he murdered in real life?"

Tom nods. "Terrible."

Maeve watches until the laugh track grates on her last nerve. "Anita said something strange when I visited her."

"Oh yeah?" He doesn't look away from the TV, even though it's an ad for Coors Light now.

"She said she didn't fall." Maeve's entire body is trembling, tiny quakes in muscles big and small. "She said Ma pushed her."

Finally, Tom looks at her. "And you believe Anita?"

"You say that like I shouldn't believe her." He doesn't seem surprised, but he also seems intent on Maeve not believing Effie pushed her.

Tom shrugs.

"Why would she say Ma pushed her if she didn't?" Maeve would like to get up to pace, but she isn't sure if her shaking legs will support her.

Tom shrugs again. "Maybe she's still trying to get you to like her better."

His words are like a giant vacuum, sucking all the air out of the room. Maeve's teeth begin to chatter.

"Are you cold?"

"It was never a competition. I loved Mom and I loved Anita."

Tom slides her a look. "I'm not sure they saw it that way."

"I was just a kid."

Hogan has returned and so Tom refocuses his attention on the TV.

She has to ask, because if she doesn't, she'll always wish she had. "Did you push Anita?"

He doesn't even look at her. "No one pushed her, Maeve. She fell. It was an accident." His voice is flat and maybe it's because he's holding back his emotions or maybe it's more than that.

Maeve nods like she believes him, even though he's not looking at her and so she can't tell if his eyes are blank, the way they always are when he's lying.

13

Maeve wants Christmas to be a thing that has happened, that they can all agree went well. Most nights, she hasn't been sleeping more than two or three hours at a time because she needs to check on her mother, even though, usually, her mother sleeps the sleep of the dead. Most nights, Maeve ends up swaying in the doorway of the guest bedroom with her eyes half closed.

Christmas won't happen without gifts and so Maeve has ventured to the Maine Mall. Paige insisted on coming—she said she could show her the boots Peter mentioned he wanted the last time he and Paige went shopping. Maeve pretends to know they went shopping and be happy about it. She also pretends to believe Paige wants to help Maeve buy things for her father, and not that she wants to talk Maeve into buying things for her.

A week ago, Paige asked Maeve to stop saying "cool." Maeve asked if she could say it if she had chills and Paige slammed the car door and stalked up to the house. Maeve should be grateful, maybe even proud, that her daughter hates her because she uses outdated slang and not because she's an alcoholic cheater or a weak-willed enabler. Instead, she resents that her daughter can't see how good she has it.

In the car, Paige talks about the sweater she might buy for Kris, something she saw at Abercrombie.

They must be serious if they're buying each other

Christmas presents. "Things seem to be going well between you two."

Paige shrugs. "I guess."

Maeve has only been to Abercrombie once and when she saw that what looked like a regular t-shirt was the same price she'd paid for her last winter coat, she left.

Maeve was hoping, irrationally, that Paige would tell her everything about Kris and their blossoming relationship without much effort on Maeve's part, but she can see that's not going to happen. "How did you guys meet?" Maeve asks.

Paige shrugs again. "He came to the movies with his friends a few times and then one of the times he asked if I wanted to hang out and so we went to a movie and then just started talking."

"Are his friends nice?"

"I guess."

As they walk into the mall, Maeve gathers Paige's hair at the nape of her neck and Paige flicks her away. She thinks of the way Anita's hair felt soft and heavy in her hands, how good it felt to be with her again, until it didn't.

If Effie pushed her, she had to have been provoked. Maybe Anita pointed out that Effie had her underwear on over her pants. Or maybe she suggested she brush her teeth, or told her Dan Rather died years ago.

There must be a thousand people in the mall, swarming like black flies in June. In the middle of the mall, Santa sits on his throne. "We should get our picture taken with him."

Paige is sixteen, and Maeve assumes she's kidding. But, when Maeve rolls her eyes, Paige stares down at her nails, painted silver, chipped at the top, thin at the edges. Maeve should suggest manicures. They went once when Paige was eleven, and it was a good day, a calm day that ended with both of them flashing their nails at Peter when they got home, laughing, and him saying they were his princesses.

"Aren't you too old for Santa?" Maeve asks. The Santa line snakes all the way to JC Penney.

When Paige shrugs, her white t-shirt lifts, revealing an inappropriate wedge of skin.

Maeve glances at the Santa line, which has hardly moved. Two kids are picking their noses. She says, "If you really want to..."

Paige, mercifully, shakes her head. "I could totally go for a coffee."

They wait in the Starbucks line for nearly fifteen minutes and have finally received their overpriced iced lattes when Maeve gets a call from Flora and feels an immediate, nearly paralyzing bolt of fear. Flora works fifteen hours a week—sometimes extra—from three until six every afternoon so Maeve can get home and start dinner without her mother shuffling out the door for a walk in her slippers. She was coming in for mornings, too, but last week, Flora confided in Maeve that she was too old and too tired to work so many hours. For now, Peter and Paige have taken over care of Effie during the day, but once school starts back up, Maeve isn't sure what she'll do. Every adult day center she's called has no openings. Maybe Dr. B will let her bring Effie to work, like Irene sometimes brings her son on snow days. Maeve will set her up next to her at the front desk with back issues of *Woman's Day* and bags of mini pretzels.

When Maeve answers, Flora says, "She's okay."

"What happened?" Maeve sits on the nearest bench, on someone's Target bag, and when the woman yanks it away,

Maeve slides over apologetically. Her coffee bubbles around the ill-fitting lid and onto her lap. Paige stares admiringly at a woman in a leather skirt the size of a dishtowel.

"I put her to bed a little after eight," Flora says.

It's eight-thirty. Paige gestures in the direction of a store that sells five hundred-dollar purses. Maeve mouths *be careful*. Paige is still sipping her iced latte. She has just reapplied glittery lip gloss so there's glitter on her straw, a dribble of coffee on her bottom lip.

It's at least ninety degrees in the mall and Maeve wipes her forehead with the back of her sleeve. She realizes too late she's spilled coffee on her sleeve and now has coffee on her forehead. She has no napkins. Flora says, "It was only ten minutes later when I heard a thump. When I got upstairs, I couldn't open her door." Flora sounds breathless and confused and Maeve worries she's having a stroke. There are so many reasons it would have been better to hire a younger caregiver for her mother, but Maeve can't deal with reason right now.

Still seated, Maeve throws her iced latte into the trash bin. A man in track pants gives her a dirty look. She wants to shout at him that she knows she isn't supposed to throw liquids into a trash bucket, but her mother might be dead and she needs her hands to keep herself from falling over.

Flora says, "She was in there shouting and finally I pushed my way in—she'd shoved the mattress off the bed and that's what was blocking the door. I went in and it was very strange. She told me to get away from him, get away—then she called me something really ugly I don't want to repeat. And then she hit me—I can't believe she meant to hit me but it seemed like she was aiming at me." Flora's voice is apologetic, and Maeve tells her it's okay even though she has no idea if it is or not. "I didn't want to call an ambulance, but there was so much blood and I'm on those blood thinners so I thought I'd better, just to be on the safe side." Maeve tries to steady herself against Christmas music and the jangle of bells and hohoho. She leans against a poster advertising Santa, even though it seems to be an entirely fatter and pinker Santa than the one who is currently being handed a baby by an elf. "They say I need stitches. And of course I can't drive myself and, I'm so sorry Maeve, they say we should go right now."

Her voice is all worn-through t-shirt. She's an old woman, taking care of another old woman. "Okay, sure. It's fine, Flora. We're on our way." It's like all the jingle bells in all the world are ringing in her skull. "We'll be home soon. I'm sure she'll be okay." She's not sure at all, but she can't very well tell Flora to apply pressure to the wound and wait. "I'm so sorry, Flora."

"Is there someone I can call? Someone who can come and sit with your mother? I tried your father but it went to voicemail."

She tells Flora not to worry. Stewart, in sunny California, will be useless. She calls Collette even though Collette has already done more than any neighbor is obligated to do. Collette sweetly says she can be at Maeve's in ten minutes and that it'll be fun to hang out with Effie for a bit. "No rush," she tells Maeve.

Paige reappears in front of Maeve, makes a gesture like pulling leaves off a tree. Maeve has no idea what she means by it so she closes her eyes. If there weren't so many people milling around, she could lay down on the bench.

A blurry version of Paige says, "Are you all right, Ma?"

Maeve stands, shimmies her purse onto her shoulder. "We need to go," Maeve says.

In their last session, Wendy told her she should think about her "long-term" plan and Maeve said the plan was for Anita to get better and go home and for her father to get back to helping her take care of Effie. "Is that realistic?" Wendy asked.

"I have hope," Maeve said after an unsustainable silence. And then she made another appointment, even though she didn't really have time for therapy.

Paige pouts like a small child. "Can I at least show you the bag I want?"

"Not now."

"Then when?"

Maeve starts to walk away, hoping Paige will follow like she used to when she was little.

Paige says, "It's on sale."

As they swish out through the mall doors, Maeve says, "I'll come back for it," even though she realizes she doesn't know which bag it is and probably can't even guess and that she'll likely forget all about the bag anyway and that, Christmas morning, Paige will be disappointed.

"I was also going to get something for Kris. He's going to be pissed if I don't get him anything and when am I supposed to come back? Ma? Are you even listening?"

Paige's voice has reached that hysterical pitch that makes Maeve want to yank her by the hair. She realizes she should ask what Paige means, why Kris will be angry, how he'll show it, if that's really the kind of relationship Paige wants to be in. She should say *language* like she used to but Paige is sixteen and Maeve doesn't really care. She thinks all of these things and can even see a different version of herself engaging in this conversation with Paige, but instead, as they cross the parking lot, Maeve says, "Where's your jacket?"

"In the car."

It's bunched in a heap on the backseat and Maeve doesn't know how she missed that Paige wasn't wearing a jacket when they walked into the mall in ten-degree weather.

Paige asks, "Can I drive?"

"Not tonight."

"You always say that."

At home, Peter, before he left for the food pantry, put a battery-operated candle in every window, even though that's usually Maeve's job. Paige bounds out of the car before Maeve can tell her there's probably blood from Flora's busted nose spattered all over the house, congealed in slimy puddles. She doesn't want Paige to be scared.

Sometime after she gets her mother to bed and cleans up the blood, Maeve will have to find Flora's broken eyeglasses and, eventually, buy her a new pair. That's really the least of her problems.

14

Maeve is fourteen and Stewart is sixteen and it is New Year's Eve. The Haverlands' have invited Effie and Tom and, by default, Stewart and Maeve, to their lake house. Stewart has plans with his friends and, even though Effie asks him to take his sister with him, he refuses.

Maeve puts on her pink Mickey Mouse sweatshirt, which Anita Haverland gave her for her birthday and which she's hardly worn since then.

"You can't wear that," Effie says.

The sweatshirt is too tight, although it's a large. Maeve has recently gained weight, upwards of fifteen pounds, which Effie tells her she'll want to "do something about" before it "becomes a real problem." Maeve's been inexplicably hungry, although Effie claims that Maeve is bored rather than hungry and that she needs to drink more water. All their cabinets have been stocked with Haverland Health bars and not much else. Maeve is wearing the sweatshirt with her jeans that pinch into her stomach, making it look, at the end of the day, like stamped Play Doh.

"What happened to your white sweater? The fuzzy one. It looks nice on you."

It's too small, which Effie must know.

"Don't cry, for goodness' sake," Effie says. "Just go change." Effie is wearing a plain black button-up blouse and jeans, but it looks nice.

Maeve doesn't change. She stays in her room until seven-fifteen and her mother has called for her three times and now it'll be too late to change. Her parents are at the door, her father in his navy ski jacket, even though they aren't a family who skis, her mother in her red wool coat. Maeve says she doesn't need a jacket.

"I don't know why you insist on embarrassing me," her mother says, which makes Maeve feel like a terrible person. She could have changed into one of Stewart's button-downs, just to please her mother, but now it's too late.

Last week, Effie asked Maeve if she was pregnant. "I'm fourteen," Maeve said. She had not, at that point, even been kissed. She kept a list of boys she wouldn't mind kissing, which she kept folded in thirds beneath her new bras. At night, she sometimes rubbed herself against her sheets until the good feeling came, the mechanics of which still mystified her. She often fell asleep feeling bad about making herself feel good.

"We should start that diet tomorrow," Effie says, latching her seatbelt. "I could stand to lose a few pounds myself."

Her mother's collarbone sticks out like chicken wings.

Maeve's father seems to not have heard them, although Effie looks over at him, anticipating he'll come to her defense, say she looks beautiful just the way she is.

The Haverlands' have outlined their house in white lights so that it looks just like a gingerbread fairytale. Anita Haverland greets them at the door. She's wearing a tight red sweater and black pants, which makes Maeve regret the casualness of the pink sweatshirt. Still, when Anita says, "That color looks beautiful with your complexion," Maeve feels pretty. Even when Effie frowns at them, Maeve keeps feeling good.

They're served duck. Effie leans over and whispers to

Maeve to eat it, even if it's greasy. Maeve doesn't find it particularly greasy, although she's so worried she won't like it, it almost doesn't matter that she does.

When Maeve reaches for more mashed potatoes, her mother stops her hand. "How about some more salad?"

Maeve doesn't take salad, but she doesn't take potatoes, either.

The adults drink pink cocktails and Maeve has ginger ale. Charlie shows her a trick in which he makes it look like he's taken his thumb off, which he's shown her before. She pretends to be delighted. After that, the talk turns to Haverland Health and the new product Charlie plans to "roll out." It's a pill, or what Charlie calls a "supplement."

"We're trying to make it smaller. Or crushable. But it'll have all the nutrition an average-sized woman needs in a day. Take one of these, and just drink water the rest of the day and the pounds will melt off."

Anita taps Effie's hand and tells her she has some Avon samples she thinks she'd like. Effie smiles like she might really like to try the new shade of lipstick or anti-wrinkle cream.

By eight, Maeve has helped clear the table and bring out dessert, which is a three-layer chocolate cake with white frosting in between each layer and which, when Effie takes a single bite of it, she closes her eyes and moans in a way that makes Maeve's cheeks flame. The Haverlands' don't believe in denial of pleasure, Charlie says. Just regulation. Self-control. Maeve eats her cake quickly, in case her mother plans to tell her not to.

After that, the adults play cards and drink more pink cocktails and Maeve wanders around the den looking at Anita's pictures. This room has wood floors and brown leather couches, and so Anita's pictures here are framed in simple black, not the fancy golden ones she has in her white living room. There's the one of sand, and another of coffee. Grass, moss, and honey are clustered together near a metal lamp in the shape of a tree branches.

Finally, tired and full, Maeve finds the Haverlands' dog, a sad-sack Bassett hound named Bailey, and sits cross-legged on the floor, stroking Bailey's ears and watching Dick Clark's Rockin' New Year's Eve.

At some point, Maeve falls asleep. When she wakes, she and Bailey are the only ones in the house. Instead of panic, she feels a kind of relief.

She hears their voices from the back deck. Probably they're out there smoking cigarettes, which they think Maeve is too stupid to know about. She rubs Bailey's belly. She read once that dogs only show their bellies when they feel completely at ease, and it pleases Maeve that she can have that effect on someone, even if that someone is a dog. She feels sleepy and wonderful and nearly dozes off. And then she hears yelling. She gets up to investigate.

Her father and Charlie Haverland stand unsteadily, arms akimbo, on the banister. The deck is twelve feet off the ground, at least, but there's a good four feet of snow below it. When Maeve opens the sliding glass door, her father is explaining to her mother that they'll definitely land in the snow. Stop being a stick in the mud, he says. He circles his arms. Effie turns away from him and sees Maeve. "Go inside so you don't see your father kill himself."

"Oh, Effie," Anita says. "You're such a worrier." Her nails are painted the hottest of the hot pinks. Maeve wishes, and almost makes herself believe, that Anita said "warrior," but that can't be right given the sickly tone of Anita's voice. It's one Maeve has never heard her use before, and it makes her want to fling her arms around her mother.

Effie puts her hand on Anita's and for a moment Maeve thinks she'll hold it, that the women will hold hands and the men will jump and it'll be a little like what Maeve imagines happened on the Titanic, but less tragic. Except that Effie takes Anita's hot-pink-nailed hand and picks it off her sleeve like it's a clot of mud. She holds it out, airborne, and then lets it drop.

The men drink shots of clear liquid. They hoot and bellow, thump their glasses down on the railing, clap each other on the back. And then they jump. Charlie Haverland leaps seconds ahead of her father and soon there's the whoomp of his landing, followed by the whoomp of her father.

It's very quiet after that and Maeve wonders if they've broken all their bones and are in a heap in the snow. She'll have to call an ambulance because her mother will be hysterical. She turns to ask Anita, who has been drinking but who doesn't seem drunk, the address for the lake house when the men start laughing.

"I pissed my pants," her father yells. Maeve isn't sure she's ever heard her father laugh before. Not like this—a kind of unstoppable laugh that should delight—but instead scares—her.

Effie has gone inside. Maeve finds her in the kitchen, eating a piece of the chocolate cake Anita Haverland claimed she made from her great-aunt's recipe. "She bought this from a bakery," Effie says. There's chocolate on her teeth. Maeve hands her a napkin and makes a motion of wiping her own teeth. "The box is in the trash. She lied about it. She lies." Her words are mashed together with alcohol and cake, and so Maeve nods even though she wants to say cake is just cake and what difference does it make if she made it or not, and Anita is an artist who doesn't have time to spend all day making cake. "You shouldn't be friends with her," Effie says. "What does she want with you, anyway? Who is friends with a kid?"

Maeve flinches as if Effie has hit her. Before Maeve can mutter any kind of response, her father comes in, wet from the waist down, smelling of cold and pee and alcohol. Charlie Haverland lends him a pair of gray sweat pants with UConn in block letters down the side of one leg and her father steps out of his wet pants, right there in front of everyone. His underwear is white and small and Maeve wants to die. Her mother says, "For God's sake, Tom." Anita Haverland tips her head back and laughs.

And then it's midnight and they watch the ball drop and Charlie and Anita kiss, her mother and father kiss, and Maeve pretends to be asleep on the couch. And then Anita throws her arms around Maeve's father and kisses him with a wet slurp on the lips and when she pulls back, she laughs and tells Effie and Charlie to "lighten up."

When they're at the car, Effie holds out her hand. "Give me the keys."

"I'm fine," Tom says.

"You're not."

"You've had as much as me." By now, he's opened the door. He's sitting in the driver's seat, fastening his belt. He seems steady enough, but Effie shakes her head.

She says, "You can kill yourself, but not us. Get out of the car, Maeve."

Maeve unbuckles her seatbelt.

"Get in the car, Effie. You're embarrassing yourself."

"You're embarrassing all of us." She looks like a little girl by the side of the car, her hair frizzed in the damp, her makeup mostly gone except for a smear of mascara under her eyes. "Let me drive."

"You can't see for shit at night."

"I'll go slow."

Effie has not gotten inside the car. She has her door open, her arm on top of it, her body leaning into the car to reason with Tom. He puts the car in reverse. "Get in."

"Don't, Tom."

She's very calm, and so is he, which makes Maeve nervous. Her whole body shakes like she's on an amusement park ride that's gone on too long. He keeps backing up and Effie trots along, backwards. She's wearing heels and the driveway has patches of ice all over it. It'll only be a matter of time before she falls, before her foot catches and she slides beneath the car and Tom runs her over and she's a bloody, crumpled mess.

Maeve begins to cry.

Effie, without audible concession, hauls herself into the car. It's an acrobatic move Maeve wouldn't have thought her capable of and she almost applauds, but thinks better of it. Effie pulls the door closed, buckles her seatbelt, and stares forward.

Tom drives slowly, up the long long curve of the Haverlands' driveway. Effie says nothing. Maeve closes her eyes because keeping them open will only make her suck her breath with fear in that way that annoys her father when they approach a curve.

The next New Year's Eve she says she's sick and her parents leave her home with canned chicken noodle soup and the phone number for the Haverlands'. The year after that she says she has plans, and the year after that, she actually has plans.

15

Paige is at Becca's, Peter is volunteering at the soup kitchen, Maeve's father is, as always, at the hospital, and Collette has taken Effie to the mall "for exercise." Maeve can't imagine how Collette will control her in a mall full of Christmas shoppers, but she's decided to shelve her worry, which is Wendy's term. Maeve rolled her eyes at the idea, but now here she is, imagining her worry in a solid blue Tupperware bin, her arms stretching it onto a shelf high enough that she'll need a chair to get it back down again.

Tonight, Maeve is going to make herself a cup of tea and then she's going to take a bath with the bubble bath she's had for five years. She borrowed a *People* from work just for this.

Maeve drops her purse on the counter and strides into the living room, which is dark except for the glow from the tree. Peter always leaves it plugged in even though Maeve told him she saw a fire safety video on how quickly a tree can ignite. She doesn't mention that video was about a live tree and not their fake and likely chemically fire-resistant tree. Peter said she sounds like her father when she worries about fire and now here they are with the tree plugged in.

Maeve is nearly all the way to the tree when she sees them. Paige's long hair falls like a sheet over her bent head. She's kneeling on the floor in front of a shadowy someone, and that someone's pants are pooled at his feet. Maeve turns away quickly as though she's the one who has been caught. She crashes into the wall, her eye connecting with the corner with so much force and so much pain that at first, she thinks her eyeball has fallen out, that it'll be on the floor, possibly rolling around, and that Paige will be mad at her for embarrassing her. Maeve tries to stay perfectly still while the pain goes on and on. She hears the rustle of pants, the hum of urgency. Finally, the pain clears to a dull throb and Maeve looks up. Paige and Kris are staring at her. Paige is standing now, as if she's been standing all along, and the boy has pulled up his pants and stands beside her with his hands folded, perhaps in prayer.

Paige says, "What are you doing here?"

The tea kettle whistles.

Paige says, "You need ice for your eye."

Maeve touches her eyes and is relieved when her fingers come back dry.

Mohawk boy exhales, but otherwise doesn't move. Perhaps he's imaginary. Perhaps none of this is real.

Paige leaves the room and returns with the gel ice pack they keep in the freezer for back aches and boxed lunches. She's tucked it in a clean dishtowel, still folded from the drawer. It's so thoughtful—*she's* so thoughtful—that Maeve wants to ask her if she's okay, but she stops herself because Paige is obviously fine. In the shuffle of Paige handing things to Maeve, Mohawk boy leaves, closing the front door gently behind himself.

Maeve holds the ice pack to her face. She closes her eyes and says, "I was going to take a bath."

She hears the squeak of Paige's feet on the stairs.

When her eye feels like it probably won't swell up, Maeve puts the ice pack back in the freezer, gets out the Febreze, and soaks the couch, the rug, and the tree skirt.

She knows she should go right now and talk to Paige about sex and vulnerability and respect and whatever else she's supposed to have already talked to her teenage daughter about. Instead, she gets out a fresh teabag, re-boils the water, and waits for her tea to steep as if she has nothing better to do.

16

Maeve is fourteen the year her father gives her mother an elaborate manicure kit. It's in a long box, wrapped in shiny red paper, and Tom hands it over, smiling in a way Maeve at first thinks might be a joke. Like it might be one of those cans of peanuts with the paper snake that jump out. Or it might be a pair of earrings wrapped in a small box, then a bigger box, and then finally this biggest box. Maeve didn't help her father pick out earrings so she's pretty sure it can't be that. Or, if it is that, they'll be the tackiest earrings on the planet—huge green baubles or glittery hoops that would sweep her mother's shoulders if she ever wore them.

Effie picks off the tape and peels back the paper with the kind of slowness that makes Maeve think she, too, is unsure about the whole thing. Effie lifts the lid, pauses, closes it.

For a heart-stuttering moment, Maeve thinks it might be Clipper's ashes. Her mother refused to pick up Clipper after he'd been cremated, saying she'd never go back to "that place" again, as if the vet had been the one in the silver sedan who didn't see him.

"What is it?" Maeve asks. Her mother hands her the box. Effie's face is doing the thing it does when Maeve brings home a test with anything less than a B—a solid line of mouth, eyebrows raised, head at an uncomfortable tilt. She's disappointed, but Maeve can't understand why.

Maeve and her father reach for the box at the same time.

"I'll take it back if you don't like it," he says.

"Take it back where?" Effie asks.

There are sixteen nail polishes, ranging from cherry to bubblegum. Maeve has never seen anything so pretty, or with so much potential. Her mother's nails are as short as a boy's, peeling along the edges, ridged on the thumbs. Effie only ever uses clear polish and that's just for special occasions. She rarely even files them. But here, in this box, are all the ways her hands could look.

Maeve picks up the pinkest one and shakes it. "I like it," Maeve says, and she can't help but be pleased by the lift of her father's mouth.

Effie looks hard at Tom "You bought this from Anita Haverland."

"I thought you'd like it," he says. He leans forward and collects discarded wrapping paper and bows into a trash bag. When he straightens, he moans. He always says his back aches from sleeping on poor-quality hotel mattresses when he travels. When Maeve was smaller, he sometimes asked her to walk on his back. She pretended his back was a mountain in a strange, somewhat clammy land. She liked that her feet had the power to heal.

Maeve reaches across her mother's lap, flips the box's lid open, and picks up the hot pink from the dead center. "Can I use this one?"

"She doesn't need the money," Effie says.

Tom shrugs. "She likes selling beauty products."

Effie laughs, but it's the laugh she uses when Stewart tells knock-knock jokes. Her father says, "I wanted to surprise you."

"Surprise!" Effie says. She says this like she's telling him to get lost. She stands so quickly the box falls off her lap and the bottles tumble out. Maeve scoops up the hot pink.

"On your toes," Effie says. She picks up the box, stuffs the polishes back in, and closes the lid. "She has her fingers in everything, doesn't she?"

Anita Haverland has pale hair that stands like a white-capped wave. When Maeve was little and visited her father at his office, Anita gave her paper from the copier and highlighters in yellow, blue, pink, and green. Until Maeve met Anita Haverland, she didn't know highlighters came in anything except yellow.

Tom hands Maeve and Stewart each a present.

"Those are from Santa," Effie says, even though neither of them believes anymore and her mother knows they don't. Maeve unwraps *Little Women* and Stewart gets a bird house kit. Maeve is genuinely pleased, although she suspects Stewart is not. He'd wanted a sketch pad and charcoal pencils. He'd written it down, but Effie probably lost the paper or couldn't find the pencils and figured woodworking would be even better.

Later, when the pancakes are sizzling on the griddle, Effie uncaps the deepest red polish. Maeve thinks she's going to concede, going to suggest they sit on the couch with their feet on an old towel on the coffee table and paint their nails. Maeve is about to offer to paint each nail a different color when her mother pours the polish into the sink. It's thick like syrup and Maeve thinks she'll stop because Tom always warns them about how they're going to clog the drain with oil or grease or even the residue from a knife used for peanut butter. Effie empties the bottle until just a drip comes out, then she tosses it into the bin beneath the sink. Before she picks up the next bottle, she turns on the tap so hot steam rises and the kitchen smells like chemicals. The next polish is reddish brown, like old blood, and Effie empties that one, then the next, then the next.

When all the bottles except for the hot pink in Maeve's pocket have been emptied and the sink is streaked like the aftermath of a steak dinner, Effie hands Maeve the box. "Is this anything you can use?" She asks.

Maeve takes the box and says thank you because it seems like her mother will stand there with it forever if she doesn't.

17

At a little past ten on Thursday morning, Maeve's father calls. Maeve tucks the phone between her ear and shoulder and hands Mrs. Winters her receipt and her appointment card for six months out.

Her father says, "What time are you picking us up?"

Maeve presses the phone to her chest and tells Mrs. Peterson that she can go right into room one.

Last night, Maeve dreamt of a sea made of yellow foam, her mother in an inner tube being pulled through it by a speeding boat. "Picking you up for what?" Maeve thinks, briefly, that he means him and Anita, but even he wouldn't stoop that low. Maeve digs the tiny notebook she's started to use to help her keep track of things out of her purse and gets as far as opening it when Irene appears at the desk with Mr. Connors, who probably needs a follow-up appointment.

Her father sighs. "Paige's concert is tonight."

Shit. "Right. It's at seven? Hold on." She sets the phone down. "Sorry about that," she says to Mr. Connors and Irene. She makes his appointment, half-listening, half-smiling. Last week, Irene brought in a miniature Christmas tree and decorated it with tiny toothbrushes. It's cute, but Maeve resents the garland made of floss because it seems like a tiny reproach of all the decorating she hasn't done. She's put up a tree at home, at least, but thinking about that only makes her think of Paige's head in Mohawk boy's lap.

When she picks up the phone again, she half hopes her father will have hung up.

He says, "You said six."

She tells him okay, thanks for the reminder.

*****

Tom and Effie are waiting for her outside when she gets there. Her father opens the back door for her mother, settles her coat around her, and buckles her in. Maeve tries to blink away the stinging tears, but he notices. "What's the matter with you?" He asks.

"Did you eat dinner?" Maeve asks.

"It's six o'clock," her father says.

Maeve assumes that means yes. Her father likes to eat at five-thirty sharp. She practices the deep inhales and long exhales Wendy has had her try. If she drove them into a tree right now, she'd at least get to go to a hospital and sleep.

"Why are you breathing funny?" Her father asks.

Maeve fishes around in her purse with one hand.

"Watch the road," he says.

Is he angry? Is he angry enough to push a woman down the stairs? Is he heartless enough to continue to visit her in her hospital room afterward and come up with a plan to blame his demented wife? Maeve doesn't think so, but she also would have, before Halloween night, sworn the affair between her father and Anita had ended more than two decades ago. It's possible she doesn't know her father at all.

"Can you find me my granola bar?" she asks. Her mother is looking out the window. Maeve sets the child locks, just to be on the safe side.

As if it might be full of snakes, Tom opens her purse and

peers through the pockets. He pulls out her lists of things to do and buy and not forget, her compact (where was it when she needed it the other day?), and her set of work keys. "You've sure got a lot of stuff in here," he says. "No granola bar, though."

Maeve cranks the radio so that "Holly Jolly Christmas" fills the car. Her mother sings along. Maeve is so hungry and tired that she thinks she might float away if not for her seatbelt. She didn't have time for breakfast, and she called her mother's doctor at lunch instead of eating the salad she made a week ago and which would probably have been slimy by now, but better than nothing. Had she not left it at work, she'd eat it now, with her fingers, brown lettuce be damned. She told the doctor about the Ajax, and he was quiet for a long time before asking Maeve if she was taking care of herself. Maeve told him she'd started therapy, which was true even though she continued to go only because she kept forgetting to cancel her appointments.

In the backseat, Effie sings along to Mariah Carey's "All I Want for Christmas."

Maeve asks, "How does she know the words to this song?"

Tom says, "I think you just drove by the school."

Maeve makes a U-turn in the middle of the street, ignoring the way her father grabs the dashboard.

*****

Peter, wearing dark blue pants and a white button-down shirt, waits for them by the gym entrance. Maeve touches her hair and frizz follows her fingers.

It's too hot in the gym for the Reindeer-appliqued sweater Maeve chose this morning when she thought she'd only be at work, where her desk is near the front door and so, from

November to April, she freezes. It's also too hot for the cream-colored wool cardigan her mother is wearing, but when she asks her mother if she'd like to take it off, her father tells her it's all she's wearing. "Better than when we started," he says and Maeve decides not to press for details.

The entire chorus—made up of kids from both the high school and middle school—sing three stanzas of "Jingle Bells," all of "Rudolph the Red-Nosed Reindeer," "Santa Claus is coming to Town," and "I Saw Mommy Kissing Santa Claus." Effie sings along with every song, even though Maeve tries to shush her because this isn't that kind of concert. Peter squeezes Maeve's hand. "What difference does it make?" He whispers. He isn't the one Paige will accuse of embarrassing her if she hears her grandmother singing.

After forty minutes, Maeve leans over and asks Peter how long this is supposed to last. Peter shrugs in what Maeve thinks is a judgmental way, as if because she isn't enjoying it, she's some kind of lesser parent. Maeve sweats a river down her back and she's so hungry she considers looking for gum under her seat.

When she can't stand the sight of one more Santa hat, Maeve leans over and whispers to Peter, "How can they get away with a Christmas concert in a public school?"

He whispers back, "It's voluntary."

For a moment, Maeve's entire field of vision turns sunspot red. Paige chose to sing in this hothouse of an auditorium the week before Christmas when Maeve has not had a full night's sleep in almost seven weeks? And Maeve had to show up even though she had a million other things she should be doing. And then Maeve reminds herself that Paige is sixteen and that she can't be expected to understand what Maeve is going through and that when she agreed to this concert, Anita hadn't fallen down the stairs. Still, Maeve nearly weeps for the night she could have had if she weren't here.

After the concert is a reception, which Maeve thinks is ridiculously sophisticated for a bunch of kids. When she asks her mother if she'd like to go home, Effie smiles and says no, she's having a lovely time. Maeve looks to her father, who surely needs a drink by now, but he just shrugs, which makes Maeve think he has a flask in his NASCAR jacket.

Maeve spots Paige across the room and, as Maeve raises her arm to wave hello, Mohawk boy swoops in and kisses Paige on the lips. Maeve turns away to see Peter fishing around under his seat. Maeve thinks he's dropped his cell phone but of course he pulls out a bouquet of roses and presents them to Paige who has stopped kissing and is now in front of them, so quickly that Maeve thinks she must have imagined the kissing. But if she were hallucinating a boyfriend for her daughter, she would wish for a boy with a normal haircut. Maeve smiles her receptionist smile.

Mohawk boy smiles back. His arm makes a kind of head-lock around Paige.

Paige wiggles out from under the chokehold and inhales the roses which must have come from the supermarket and surely have no smell.

Maeve is about to ask if Kris's family is here when Maeve's father asks if she's seen Effie. It's only then Maeve looks around and doesn't see her mother. She was here a moment ago, beside her, singing the chickadee song, and now she isn't anywhere Maeve can see. The room goes dim and swaying. It's thirty degrees out and her mother is wearing thin socks and slip-on shoes and how long does it take frostbite to settle in? Maeve is about to interrupt Peter and Paige and their self-congratulatory this and that about the "performance," when she sees her mother, over in the corner by the coffee setup, talking to Collette who is wearing what Maeve hopes is a fake fur coat.

As Maeve gets closer, she hears Collette and her mother singing "Jingle Bells." Collette winks at Maeve and Maeve resists stroking the coat, which looks alarmingly real.

Collette was thirty when she moved in next door to Tom and Effie, which Maeve thought was old. And now, thirty years later, she seems young to Maeve, especially standing next to Effie, who looks baffled by all the people moving about.

"Are you ready to go, Ma?"

Effie turns, smiling. "I haven't seen you in years."

Maeve laughs to make it look like she thinks this is all very funny. "It's me, Ma. Maeve." She gestures to her reindeer sweater, as if her mother will recognize that, at least.

"Oh," her mother says. "You've done something different with your face."

Collette laughs and Maeve laughs because it would be too disruptive to sit on the floor and cry. She links her arms through her mother's. "Come with me."

Effie shakes her off. "No thank you." And then, "I thought I saw that woman with the—" she gestures a French twist at the back of her head.

Collette, over Effie's head, mouths: *Anita.*

Maeve's heart misses a full three beats before it starts back up at a gallop. "I don't know, Ma. I didn't see anyone like that." Maeve tries taking Effie's arm again but this time Effie swats her away. "We have to go now, Ma."

Effie leans in, her mouth inches from Maeve's, and says with more viscousness than Maeve has ever heard from her "I don't even know who you are."

Maeve steps back, stumbles, and catches herself on a stranger's arm. "Sorry," she says as she rights herself and tries to catch her breath.

Collette raises her eyebrows at Maeve as she gently takes Effie's arm. "We were just headed that way. Why don't we all walk together?"

And just like that, Effie comes.

In the car, her mother continues to sing until her father says he can hardly think with all that noise. "That's the song I was asking you about," Maeve says. As Maeve pulls around the front of the school, Paige emerges, arm linked through Mohawk boy's.

Her mother says, "That boy lost half his hair."

Her father laughs and Maeve can't help but laugh, too.

18

Mild Brook is a single-story brick building, u-shaped, with a parking lot in both the front and back. They've wrapped every picture and mirror to look like a present which, instead of making Maeve feel festive, makes her feel like she's inside Santa's sack.

"This is nice," Peter says.

It's nice in the way a post office is nice—more or less clean with a sense of efficiency, but not somewhere you'd want to stay for any length of time. The white floors shine with so much audacity that Maeve has to squint.

"It's clean," Peter says.

Maeve lets go of his hand. It's obvious Effie needs more care than Maeve can give her, but that doesn't mean Maeve has to like it.

They tell the cardigan-wearing receptionist they're here for a tour. Maeve thinks hysterically about Gilligan's Island. She imagines herself on a boat, sliding across the shiny floors. They may never get home. Maybe they can build a phone out of wrapping paper. She and Wendy are working on a technique in which Maeve thinks of her breath as a folded fan, expanding and contracting with evenness—no kinks or hitches. She tries it now, but her fan won't open.

Cindy-the-social-worker introduces herself with the smile of a used car sales woman. Maeve and Peter follow her down another overly decorated hallway.

Peter squeezes Maeve's hand. "Give it a chance."

Cindy enters a series of numbers on a keypad. The numbers are embossed beneath the keypad, and Maeve finds the obvious point of this—that people are meant to be kept in and not out—upsetting enough to bring tears to her eyes. When Cindy swings open the door, she stands aside and ushers Maeve and Stewart in. There's a man by the door, tall, big-handed, and Cindy smiles so wide Maeve feels the pain in her own cheeks. Cindy says, "Hiya, Dwight. Let's just head over this way." She's smooth and careful, the way a park ranger might be with a bear.

Dwight turns convivially in the direction Cindy has suggested.

Peter squeezes Maeve's hand in the one-two-three that used to mean "I love you" and now means something like "Don't freak out." Dwight turns back as if he's rethought his exit and mutters something Maeve can't understand. Maeve looks at Cindy, but Cindy is making eye contact with Dwight. She takes his arm, sleek and smooth like a tour guide. There's something that might be chocolate pudding on Dwight's shirt.

Once Dwight lumbers off in the direction of a couch, Cindy sweeps her arms wide. "This is the hub," she says. She game-show points to a cluster of stiffly upholstered couches and a rickety piano. Maeve thinks about the hub outside her dorm room at the University of Maine. She thinks of the pizza she ate there with the other girls who claimed they didn't want to go to parties but who in truth weren't invited and weren't bold enough to just show up. She thinks of how lonely she was in those years and she hates the thought of her mother feeling that way.

"Lots of light," Peter says. He gestures toward the row of

windows as if Maeve needs clarification on the source of the light.

Cindy plucks an Activity Calendar from the bulletin board. "We have a lot going on here."

Maeve glances at the calendar. "What if someone doesn't like Bingo?" Three times a week, Bingo is offered. Twice, Pokeno, which is a card version of Bingo.

Cindy blinks at her. "Most everyone likes Bingo."

"Your mother likes Bingo," Peter says.

Maeve shrugs. Her mother used to go to Bingo at the VFW every Saturday night when Stewart was old enough to babysit Maeve. Saturday nights were her father's poker nights. But the last time Maeve pulled out the little Bingo game she bought when Paige was six or seven, her mother put the plastic red discs in her mouth and sucked them like candy. Maeve says, "My mother likes Scrabble and rummy. She likes to sing."

Cindy smiles harder. "We offer sing-a-longs at least once a week."

Last week, Maeve had to fish two Scrabble tiles—an E and a T—out of the space between her mother's cheek and gums. Her old mother never ate hard candy for fear of breaking a tooth.

A woman in a wheelchair rolls into the hub, lifts her shirt, and wipes her face. She isn't wearing a bra and her breasts remind Maeve of beanbags.

Peter studies the calendar. He says, "They have dog visits." His voice is all careful hope, like lulling a stray cat to a can of tuna.

Powder-scented room spray wafts into the hub. It's meant to cover the smell of shit, but it fails.

Cindy touches Peter's arm. "Does your Mom respond to

animals?"

Maeve doesn't want to talk about Clipper or how he was given to her mother more than thirty years ago as a balm for an affair that apparently never ended. Clipper, run over by a car, a death her mother grieved as much as she grieved the loss of her sister. To Cindy, Maeve says, "Do you know the Chickadee song?"

Cindy tips her head, the way she must if a resident asks her the way to the bus stop. She says, "How does it go?"

Without pause, Maeve sings: "Chickadee-chick-cha-la-cha-la-anna-cabana-can't you see? Chickadee-chick is me."

Peter and Cindy both stare at her, Peter undoubtedly surprised she has burst into song, Cindy surprised at the mishmash of sounds that, now that they're out in public, are clearly not a real song. Will the people who work here or the people who live here or the people who visit tell her mother it's not a real song? Will they, like mean girls in middle school, make fun of her?

Maeve looks away even though Cindy is still smiling, or maybe because Cindy is still smiling. Maeve wonders how she can keep it up. She wonders if, when she goes home, Cindy smashes plates against her kitchen floor.

Maeve asks, "Would you call me if my mother woke up in the middle of the night and didn't know where she was?"

Cindy doesn't smile at this, but she looks thoughtful in a way that seems put on. "We'd reassure and reorient her," she says.

"What if that doesn't work? What if she's still upset?"

"Sometimes the doctor prescribes a medicine to be taken as needed, just to calm a person down when they're very, very agitated."

This doesn't make Maeve feel any better. She wants Peter

to protest, to say something about the problem of over-medicating, but his face is all pleasant agreement.

Cindy ushers them along, through this hub and into the next, which has the same plasticky pastel-striped couches, the same beige blinds, the same white floors. She leads them through the dining room, past the living room with the high ceilings and framed Monet prints. She leads them off the locked Dementia unit, down more white halls, through a cloud of stewed tomatoes and pee. They finish in the Activity Room, where a young woman cuts out snowflakes from blue construction paper.

"This is Raine," Cindy says.

Rain rain go away. Raine waves and Maeve waves back and she remembers waving to Paige in her kindergarten room, cutting out similar snowflakes.

Maeve turns to Cindy. "Do you have Twinkies here?"

"Not regularly," Cindy says. She straightens one of the snowflakes taped to door of the Activity Room. In the process, she tears a corner, and Maeve thinks she'll ask Raine for tape, or confess what she's done, but she just leaves it, dangling.

"What about Yodels?" Maeve asks.

"We can probably bring them in," Peter says. "They can keep them at the nurses' station and give her one whenever she asks."

Maeve hates him for his reasonableness. "That's terrible," she says. "That she can't just have one whenever she wants. That she has to *ask*."

Peter shoots her a questioning glance. "Don't you keep them where she has to ask you at home?"

Maeve glares at him. "My mother isn't ready for this," she says.

Cindy nods with all the affability she's had for the tour. "The waiting list can be long," Cindy says. "And you can always tell us she's not ready if we happen to have an opening before it's time."

Peter inhales in a way that Maeve knows means he wants her to be reasonable. "It's just a list," he says when she finally looks at him.

*****

In the car, Maeve thinks about all the ways in which she'll say no when Cindy calls to tell her they have an opening. *She's not ready. It's not time. Go to hell.*

Peter says, "It's not a bad place."

Maeve says nothing.

Peter says, "She's getting harder to handle."

Gently, Peter says, "I don't want to make you do anything you aren't ready to do, but it might be a good idea to put her on the list, just so we'll be ready."

Maeve says, "She's my mother. I owe her more than a shared bedroom in a place that smells like diarrhea."

To his credit, Peter doesn't say that she also owes Paige a mother who is doing a better job than she's currently managing. Maeve's not sure what she'd say to that.

After a while, she asks, "What's going to happen if Anita tells someone—besides me—that she thinks my mother pushed her down the stairs?"

Peter glances at her. "You think she will?"

"I don't know. Maybe." Maeve closes her eyes. "I don't know why she told me."

"I don't know what good would come out of her telling anyone," Peter says. As if good is all that ever matters.

19

When Maeve is fifteen, her mother tells her father they'd be better off without him. It's not the first time she's said this.

Effie waits for him at the front door and as soon as he opens it, she pushes him back out. Spittle flies out of her screaming mouth. Tom twists his body and stumbles on the steps, sliding down one, but catching himself before he cracks his head against the concrete.

Effie says, "I'm not going to be made a fool of."

It was Maeve who told her mother that her father had gone with Anita Haverland to an exhibit of her photographs. "Like a date," Maeve said. She'd said it viciously, victoriously. She added, "In case someone says something about seeing them together. This way you can act like you knew."

And then, "You hated it the last time you went to that gallery. Dad was probably just doing you a favor."

Effie made a ha ha ha sound that made Maeve think of throwing up.

Now, Effie flings herself at Tom fist-first. "You said you were working late." She yanks on his golden tie as if she might strangle him. They're on the porch and Effie, all one hundred and ten pounds of her, pulls him down, onto the lawn.

Maeve, upstairs, begins to cry. "Don't, don't, don't," she says. She means both: don't make a spectacle in front of the neighbors—god, what if Collette is watching—and don't kill him.

"I didn't want to upset you," he says. He rolls on top of her, kneels so that one leg is on either side of her. He doesn't put his hands to her throat, as if this makes him the better person. He leaves them by his side, loose, casual. It's all okay here.

Maeve is above them, in her bedroom, with the window open and the lights out.

"Don't patronize me," Effie says. And then Tom gets up, stares at Effie for a moment, and turns and walks back down the driveway to his car. It's still ticking its way to cooling down. He gets in and Effie does nothing until he backs out of the driveway. Then she screams and screams that he's no good, that he never loved her, that she hopes he dies.

That night, Maeve locks herself in the bathroom with the intention of killing herself. She swallows a handful of Tylenol and then writes her suicide note. She says she's sorry. She says she knows she's a terrible person. She read somewhere that most people who are serious about suicide don't leave a note.

She watches herself cry and take one Tylenol after the other, entirely aware that it would be more dramatic if she didn't have to put her head under the faucet for a mouthful of water and then lift her head and throw it back like a horse. Some girls at school dry-swallow pills for cramps or head-aches, but Maeve has never been able to swallow even a baby aspirin without a huge gulp of water.

Maeve waits to feel something. She's expecting sleepiness or dizziness or a floating sensation. She feels nothing except waterlogged. Neither her mother nor Stewart come looking for her. There are two bathrooms in the house, so they don't need this one. No way would her father ever come look for her, even if he was home.

After ten Tylenol, Maeve leaves the bottle, pockets the suicide note, and knocks on her mother's door. "I just tried to kill myself," she says.

Effie is on the bed on her back, still in her blouse and shoes. She says, "Please don't start with me, Maeve."

20

Her father says he'd like to take her mother out for lunch. He says they always go out for a nice lunch around Christmas.

"This isn't always," Maeve says. Maeve is eating crystalized honey from the very bottom of the jar. Collette brought over the honey because her friend's husband or someone keeps bees and Collette has jars and jars of honey lined up in her pantry and just before Christmas is when the old version of Maeve used to bake cookies and Collette thought Maeve could use honey in a recipe for some kind of fancy thin cookie rolled and filled with cream.

But this version of Maeve hasn't even thought about cookies.

This version of Maeve has eaten all the honey from the jar. It was too cold in the pantry, hence the crystallization and the scraping, but Maeve doesn't care.

Maeve remembers a picture Anita Haverland did of honeycomb. There were all these nooks that made Maeve think of places to hide.

"Maybe Dimillo's," her father says. Her father's eyes are glassy and red, as if he's been crying. Or drinking.

Maeve licks honey off her wrist.

Tom says, "We always went to DiMillo's. We used to go shopping afterwards."

Maeve can't imagine her father going willingly in and out of the small, expensive shops in the Old Port.

"I can drop her off at the door," her father says. He's thinking of the ice, of the crusty snow. He's not thinking Effie might wander off to get a closer look at a seagull and fall into the bay.

The honey has hit the back of Maeve's throat and clings there with a sickening sweetness. "She wanders. You can't leave her alone." He, of all people, should know that.

Tom looks surprised. "She'd stay put if you told her to stay put, wouldn't she?"

Maeve shakes her head. "Not anymore." She'd tried this a few weeks ago, dropping her off at the entrance of Hannaford and telling her to wait while she parked the car. By the time Maeve got out of the car, her mother was already gone and she'd spent the next thirty minutes frantically searching for her. She'd finally found her talking to a cardboard elf.

Tom says, "Maybe you could drive us in? That way, you could drop us both at the door. Problem solved." Her father looks old and sad, not much like a man who could push his lover down the stairs and keep quiet about it.

There's a scrim of honey along the bottom of the jar and Maeve rolls up her sleeve and goes after it with her middle finger.

"Tell me what happened with Anita."

"She was over at the house—"

"You've been seeing her all these years."

He sighs. "It's complicated, Maeve."

She scrapes the little lip on the honey jar with her nail, then scrapes her nail with her teeth.

"You've got some—" Her father gestures to the honey collected on her wrist and the cuff of her sleeve. "She's always liked the Christmas tree downtown," he says.

She's about to say fine, lunch sounds great when the honey

jar slips out of her grip and shatters on the linoleum. Maeve would have thought it might not, that it might bounce, that the linoleum would be soft enough to cushion the fall.

*****

Maeve drops her parents at the door to DiMillo's. "You're not coming in?" Her mother asks.

Maeve shakes her head. "I'm going shopping. You have a nice lunch with Dad." Even if he pushed Anita, he wouldn't hurt Effie. Not in a crowded restaurant, anyway.

This is the story that makes the most sense: Tom and Anita were arguing and he pushed her and she fell. They've decided together to blame Effie, who can't defend herself. But why would Anita protect Tom? Or, if she really wanted to protect him, why wouldn't she just say she fell? It has to be that Anita wants Maeve to be afraid of her mother. As if she didn't do enough damage to their relationship for all of Maeve's childhood.

Maeve isn't going shopping. She should. She could. Instead, she's going to sit in her car and listen to NPR. She'll watch people. She brought *Anna Karenina*, which she has never read but feels like she should, even though it's a fat, ambitious book under the best of circumstances.

After ten minutes, she hasn't managed a single paragraph. Maybe she'll nap. When Paige was a baby, Maeve would sometimes drive to Crescent Beach, park, crack her window an inch, and fall asleep with her head tilted up to the sun while Paige napped in her car seat.

She calls Paige. "Do you want to go for a walk on the beach tomorrow?" Tomorrow, she only works from ten until two and it stays light out until four-thirty at least, so they'll have time.

Not a lot of time, but some. She likes the beach best at this time of year—uncrowded and with agitated surf.

Paige hesitates. "With Gram?"

Maeve feels the tug of all the people she's supposed to be—mother, daughter, wife, employee, human being and citizen of the world. "Just us."

"Sure," Paige says. And then sweetly, "It's a date."

After she hangs up, Maeve realizes she's starving. She could go to a bar. When was the last time she went a bar? A glass of wine, some French fries. But then, she can't take wine to go. She could drink it fast at the bar, but how would that look? She ends up calling DiMillo's for an order of fries to go. She has her water bottle in the car.

At the doorway, she hears her mother laugh before she sees them. Maeve turns toward the laugh and sees her father standing behind her mother. He ties the back of her plastic lobster bib and then leans down, brushes the hair from her neck, and kisses her nape. Her mother's smile turns full volt.

DiMillo's is an actual boat, and when Maeve starts to sway, she tells herself it's the upheaval of a wave. How can such a tender man also be a man who carried on an affair for years, probably decades? Is it possible to love two women? Does it matter if it breaks one of their hearts?

Wendy likes to remind her that the only two people who can really know a marriage are the two people in it. Maeve doesn't have the energy to find a therapist who doesn't speak in dogmas.

Maeve hurries to the bathroom. She sits on the toilet and counts to a hundred in order to get her mind to stop tripping through every time her father lied to her mother. *I'm working late, I'm at a conference, You're imagining things, There's nothing between us, You need to trust me, You know I'd never jeopardize our family.*

But then, why hadn't he just left? Maybe it was Anita who wouldn't leave Charlie and Tom who didn't want to be alone and so stayed with Effie. But then why is he here now?

Someone comes in and uses the stall next to her and, based on the woman's humming, Maeve's afraid it might be her mother. It isn't. Her mother has on her brown waterproof ankle boots today and this woman is wearing nonsensical pink suede loafers.

At the sink Maeve fills her hands with water and pats her face then dries it with the brown paper towels that smell faintly of mushrooms. She pays for her fries and sits in the lobby, mostly obscured by DiMillo's Christmas tree with its ornaments of lobster traps and lobsters and tiny felted Maines. She eats and watches her parents through the branches. They look like a normal couple. Old, happy, weathered. Her father has ordered lobster. Maybe her mother asked for it. She used to love lobster. He cracks it for her and, with her fingers, she digs out the meat and drags it through butter.

"Do you need ketchup?" The hostess asks Maeve.

Maeve shakes her head. She doesn't want her father to hear her, to look up, to see her seeing them.

He splits her mother's baked potato, spreads butter on her bread, flags down the waitress when Effie drops her fork. He finishes one drink and orders another, then another before that one is gone. Her mother drinks white wine. Maeve isn't sure she can have wine with her medication, but she isn't going to stop her.

Maeve can't hear them, but they're talking. Through the branches of the tree, she can see her father's mouth moving, his hands gesturing. Maeve can only see the back of her mother's head and her profile, but from that she can tell she's smiling. She thinks she hears her mother say, "This is very nice."

She thinks of Anita Haverland, bleeding at the bottom of the stairs.

When the bill comes, Maeve scoots out and has the car at the front door when her parents emerge, her mother still with the shine of butter on her chin.

"It's cold in here," her father says. "Didn't you keep the car running? You aren't one of those environmental freaks, are you?"

"How was your lunch?" Maeve asks.

"Very nice," Effie says. Maeve opens the glove compartment and hands a tissue to her mother. When her mother simply holds the tissue, Maeve's father gestures at his own chin until she understands and wipes daintily.

"We had lobster," he says.

"Lobster!" Effie says. "Where did you get that kind of money?"

"You had lobster, too," he says.

"No, I didn't."

"You were with me, Effie. We both had the lobster." His voice has gone hard.

She says, "Maybe you were with someone else."

"It was ten minutes ago."

"I don't like when you go out without me. Was it with that Haverland woman?" Her mother's tone has gone vicious, like a cornered dog.

"Anita is in the hospital," Tom says. He's clenching his teeth. If anyone pushed anyone, it had to be her father.

Maeve says, "It doesn't matter, Dad. You guys had a good

time."

"I spent almost seventy dollars," he says.

"I think I'd remember that," Effie says.

Tom's face has gone red and damp. Maeve turns down the heat. "But it was a nice meal?"

Her father sighs, presses his head against the window. "For me it was."

21

"I don't think it's a good idea," Stewart says.

"She's an old woman, Maeve. With a head injury," he says.

"I don't get what you're trying to accomplish," he says.

"Let sleeping dogs lie," he says.

"Isn't it 'lay'?" Maeve asks while she launches herself out of the car and across the hospital parking lot. She slips on a patch of black ice, catches herself, and tweaks her back in the process. A less-determined version of herself would take the slip as a sign to turn back, but Maeve doesn't turn back.

Stewart says, "I think you're only going to hurt yourself, Maeve."

"I love you," she says. "I have to hang up now."

Wendy had also asked her what she wanted to accomplish by seeing Anita again.

"Closure," Maeve said.

Wendy tipped her head.

And then, "Answers."

Wendy had tried to get Maeve to say more about what she might feel when she confronted Anita, but Maeve didn't want to think about that and she ran out the clock by talking about their tour of Mild Brook and how, sure, it seemed like a good place but it wasn't home and what would happen if her mother woke up in the middle of the night and called for her?

Wendy said the staff has likely encountered that before and are probably trained to handle it. Wouldn't Maeve agree?

Maeve did agree, half-heartedly, and then time was up.

Maeve's father has a doctor's appointment today, which is why Maeve has come to the hospital now, when she knows she won't be interrupted.

Anita is asleep when Maeve gets to her room and she looks almost dead. Her skin is gray, her breaths shallow. Her lovely hair that Maeve can still feel the echoes of in her fingertips is splayed across the pillow, damp with sweat or grease.

The kindest thing to do would be to leave. But Maeve sits in her father's chair. She hasn't brought a book, so she closes her eyes and listens to the hum of voices and footfall and beeping machines. She must doze off, because she opens her eyes to the sensation of being watched and sees Anita's gray-blue eyes staring at her.

Anita smiles thinly. "Back again."

Maeve sits upright. She won't stand, won't hover over Anita's bed like she's threatening her. She says, "Have you told anyone else what you told me? About my mother."

Anita narrows her eyes. "You mean that she pushed me."

Maeve will not flinch. "Yes."

Anita rolls her head from side to side. "Your father knows, of course. He saw it happen."

Maeve's mouth has gone so dry it feels almost chapped. She sucks her tongue to generate enough saliva to say, "He says you fell."

Anita barks a raspy laugh and Maeve thinks, for the first time since she got here, that Anita may not be on the mend. "And you believe him?"

"I should believe you instead?"

"When have I ever lied to you, Maeve?"

And this, Maeve realizes as her heart squeezes, is why she's really come. "All the time, I think. My whole childhood. You used me. Made me believe we were friends when, really, I was just an excuse. A way for you to get closer to my father."

Anita blinks at her.

If they were standing at the top of the stairs to her parents' basement, Maeve might push her, just for the look of absolute distaste on Anita's face right now.

Maeve doesn't allow herself to sink back against the chair, which is warm from the sun and might feel like a tender embrace.

"I cared about you," Anita says finally.

"You were mostly just using me."

Anita lifts her head and shakes it. "That's harsh, Maeve. You sound like your mother."

"Leave my mother out of this." The fury Maeve feels makes her dizzy. Still, she keeps her back straight, even as the room blurs and tilts.

"I don't see how we can. That's what this is all about, isn't it? You feel guilty that you loved me, respected me, admired me. And you didn't feel much or any of that for your own mother. And now, when you see what she's capable of—" Anita gestures to her bandaged head, "—you're defensive. It's uncomfortable, I understand that, but you're being unreasonable."

I'm an adult, Maeve reminds herself. *I'm a grown-up woman who does not have to be made to feel like a chastised little girl.* "Why didn't you leave Charlie? Why didn't my father leave my mother? If you two loved each other so much—" Maeve has to stop because she can feel the fracture in her voice and she will not burst into tears in front of Anita Haverland.

Anita shrugs. "Your father knew your mother wouldn't take it well if he left her and, despite what you seem to think, he cares about her. He never wanted to hurt her."

"And you were fine with the whole thing? Of being his mistress forever?"

Anita has lowered her head back onto the pillow and, the longer Maeve stays, the more it looks like she's sinking into the bed. "I had Charlie to think about." Anita closes her eyes.

Maeve stands and gathers her purse. "I was just a kid, Anita. You shouldn't have put me in the middle of this."

Without opening her eyes, Anita turns toward Maeve's voice. "I gave you something you were missing out on at home. You were happy. Don't forget that."

22

For Maeve's sixteenth birthday, Anita Haverland buys her a camera. It's a Cannon Sure Shot, and Maeve can hardly restrain herself from starting right then and there and photographing the remnants of the cake her mother spent all day making and decorating.

"Why would she buy you something so expensive?" Effie asks.

The camera had been wrapped in iridescent green paper. It's a color that echoes the peas Anita sometimes photographs, which strikes Maeve as clever. Maeve picks carefully at the tape and folds the paper along its creases. The camera is heavy, but she doesn't want to put it on the coffee table where their mugs and crumb-covered plates are still strewn.

Stewart runs a finger around the edge of his plate before Effie whisks them into a pile and into the sink. Her father says, "I was going to have another piece of cake."

"You don't need another piece of cake," Effie doesn't turn around when she says this so she misses the face he makes at her back.

"Well, you don't," Maeve says.

"You don't, either," her father says.

Maeve sucks in the stomach which rolls over her jeans like dough.

Effie, returning, says, "Did you ask her to buy that for you?"

"No." She didn't ask, but last month Anita asked her if

she'd been practicing what they worked on with lighting and angles and Maeve said her cheap Kodak wouldn't do much besides let her look through the view finder and snap the picture. She'd said this as a way of saying yes, that she was practicing, but that she wasn't very good. Anita said she should ask for a better camera for her birthday and Maeve told her her parents would never buy her a camera because they were paying for driver's ed and her mother made it clear that was her one and only birthday present.

Now, her father leans over the camera. "It's just like the one Anita has."

"It's way too much." Her mother wipes the coffee table with a damp paper towel.

Her father says, "Anita's very generous."

He says this casually, but Effie looks wounded. "It's easy to be generous when you have plenty of money." She scrubs so hard at a spot, which Maeve thinks is just part of the table, that the paper towel tears and bits of it lodge in the grooves of the wood.

"I think it's because I help Anita with her photographs," Maeve says.

Effie says, "I don't want to have to start exchanging birthday gifts with them. There'll be no end to it."

Effie makes it sound like they're going to exchange body organs and Maeve rolls her eyes at Stewart, facing away from her parents so they don't send her to her room.

When Anita Haverland asked Maeve about if she'd been practicing, she was leaning in close, showing Maeve how to look through the viewfinder. She smelled, as always, of oranges, and Maeve was tempted to ask about her perfume. She's gone three times to the perfume area at JC Penney and still can't figure it out.

"Make sure you write a thank-you note," her mother says. She's given up on the table and is collecting wrapping paper into a huge trash bag. Her parents gave her socks and a sweater the color of the insides of a cantaloupe. It's not a color she thinks will look good on her, but she'll wear it to school tomorrow anyway. Stewart gave her a joke book, which Maeve figures her mother bought her and put Stewart's name on, and which she will never open.

"I will," Maeve says.

"Do we even have any thank-you notes?"

"I can make a thank-you note," Maeve says.

Her mother sighs. "We'll get some tomorrow."

Maeve is supposed to go to Anita's tomorrow. They had set it up that Maeve would come every other day to help Anita finish the series she was doing on fruits that represent a color. She still had peach, grape, and raspberry left. She knows better than to say this to her mother.

23

At six in the morning on December twenty-third, Maeve has showered, poured a to-go cup of coffee, and is almost out the door—she would have been out the door if her keys had been in her purse and not in the freezer—when she realizes her father is sitting in the recliner in the living room. The TV is off and he's staring at the lights on the tree, a strand of which has gone out.

"I didn't know you were here," Maeve says.

Her father startles, but doesn't turn. Maeve assumes he's here so he can greet Stewart and Natalie when Maeve gets back with them. Maeve tries not to resent that she's hardly seen her father for weeks, but for Stewart he shows up.

Tom says, "She died."

For a second, Maeve thinks he means Effie. That her mother has died in her sleep and, terribly, for only a flash, Maeve is relieved. But then she hears the toilet flush and remembers she's just checked on her mother, who was asleep and breathing.

He means Anita, then.

Maeve stays where she is, behind her father's chair, leaning against the wall. Her muscles feel like they've turned to jelly. She remembers the softness of Anita's hair through her fingertips that first day she saw her, after so many years, and then her gray, putty-like pallor yesterday. Can hatred kill a person? "What happened?"

Her father's shoulders raise and lower in a slow shrug. "Brain bleed, they say." He lifts a mug to his lips and Maeve can smell from here that it isn't coffee.

She can hear the hum of the Christmas lights. Was she dying yesterday while Maeve was telling her she was an awful person to manipulate a child into being her fan club of one?

He says, "I thought we were out of the woods when she woke up, but…" He shakes his head, then takes a long drink from his mug.

He's crying. Maeve can see the wet on his cheeks. The last time she saw him cry was when his own mother died. Maeve was only six and the sight of her father crying now is as shocking as it was then.

Maeve wants to feel sorry for him but this is all his fault. She doesn't care who Anita claims pushed her or if, like Tom says, she was startled and fell. Tom is to blame for her being at the Ever-yellow to begin with and so he's responsible for her death. Paperwork my ass, Maeve thinks. She was at the Ever-yellow to see him and maybe they had an argument or maybe she just stumbled, but whatever happened, she wouldn't have fallen if she weren't there. As to what Anita said about Effie pushing her, that was the talk of a woman with a brain injury, or a woman trying to protect the man she's been having an affair with for more than forty years. Or a mean, horrible person who, even now, wants to turn Maeve against her mother. If they loved each other so much, why couldn't they have just let their spouses go? Why carry on deceiving everyone? Maeve crosses her arms. "Why are you here?" It's unkind, and Wendy-in-head shakes her head.

Tom looks up, mug still at his lips. "I didn't want to be alone."

"So you came to my house, where your wife is sleeping upstairs, and wallowed in pity for the death of your mistress." Maeve's glad Peter isn't awake to hear her. The hurt on her father's face makes her both furious and deeply ashamed and she takes a breath. "I'm going to get Stewart and Natalie."

Tom nods and sips.

Effie shuffles into the kitchen. She's fully dressed—in shorts Maeve has never seen but which might be her father's—and a gray t-shirt with a logo for the car dealership where her father bought the Toyota.

Effie says, "Can I come with you?"

She says it like she knows Maeve is going to get Stewart. Maeve hesitates.

"I can't handle her right now," Tom says.

Maeve wants to knock the Captain's out of his hand. "She's your wife," she hisses at him. To her mother, she smiles. "Sure." Peter and Paige are still sleeping.

Maeve thinks about asking her mother to put on warmer clothes, but she doesn't have time and they won't need to get out of the car.

It's been years since Maeve's been to the airport, and she takes one or two wrong turns and then they're near the mall, stuck in a line of cars turning left.

Effie says, "I don't think I had breakfast."

No one will let Maeve get in the right lane, which is where she needs to be. She rolls down her window, holds out her arm and circles her hand in what she hopes is a gesture that indicates she's sorry, but someone—how about you nice lady with the curly hair and beret?—needs to let her in. It's Christmas, after all. The curly-haired lady inches forward. Maeve changes her hand signal to something unmistakably un-Christmas-y.

"I'm cold," Effie says. "Aren't you cold?"

Finally, they get to the airport and park. Maeve texts Stewart and beeps when she sees him and Natalie sweep out the revolving doors, her brother tall and tanned and easy in his body, the way he's always been, and Natalie wild-haired and in a skirt that looks like it could double as a blanket. It might actually be a blanket.

Effie says, "She needs a hairbrush."

Maeve laughs.

"I think they're coming here," Effie says. "Do you know them?"

"It's Stewart and Natalie," Maeve says. Maybe Stewart will finally see how much more confused Effie is, how much more help Maeve needs. It's unrealistic, Maeve knows, to think he and Natalie will leave their jobs and friends and house and move back to Maine to help her. Still, in her deepest fantasy, that's exactly what they do.

As they approach, Maeve gets out of the car to help them with their suitcases. Effie gets out, too, even though Maeve tells her they're all set, they can handle the bags.

"I thought we were getting Grace," Effie says, and her voice is filled with accusation.

Maeve shakes her head. She isn't supposed to say that Grace is dead, that she died more than twenty years ago of ovarian cancer, that, before she died, Effie filled Grace's freezer with chicken soup when she was sick because she was a good, devoted sister. Once, Tom put on Grace's blonde wig and made them all hysterical with laughter.

Or, maybe she *is* supposed to say it, to re-orient her mother. She can never remember what she's supposed to do with reality when reality is something she, too, would rather forget.

"Where are your clothes?" Natalie exclaims when she hugs Effie.

Effie looks startled by the hug.

"It's warm in the car," Maeve says. She should have at least made her mother put on a coat.

She should tell Stewart right away that Anita has died, but he's laughing and kissing Effie and lying about how good Maeve looks, and she just can't.

Effie pulls away and begins to walk toward the airport so that Maeve has to drop Natalie's bag and jog after her. "This way, Mom." She tugs on Effie's arm.

"I forgot something," Effie says. She's shivering. Maeve takes off her coat and drapes it around her, fastens two of the buttons.

"Come this way," Maeve says.

Stewart, behind them, laughs. "How much trouble do you think she can get into?"

Maeve wants to tell him she might be able to push a woman down the stairs, if you believe Anita.

Effie shakes her off and turns toward the airport. Maeve follows. Her mother, who seems so shuffling, so frail, is walking with enough purpose that Maeve has to trot to keep up. She could tackle her, but she'd likely break something, possibly everything. She could get Stewart to help drag their mother back to the car. Or carry her. Or, she could let her go into the airport and get stopped by security and explain god only knows what to them.

Natalie says, "Where are you guys going?"

They're almost to the glass doors when Stewart catches up. "Hey, Ma." He kisses Effie's cheek and she turns, beams at him.

"Where did you come from?" She asks. "Did you see a woman with a twisty thing for a hairdo? I saw her go in."

He smiles like this is great, like they're kids and Effie is joining them for a game of hide-and-seek. "No," Maeve says as Stewart says, "Maybe."

"The car's this way," he says. He links his arm through hers and steers her toward the parking lot.

Maeve wonders how quickly she could disappear into the airport. Do you need a passport to fly if you aren't flying internationally? She has her license and credit card. She could go somewhere dark and humid. A forest on an island. St. Thomas or St. John. Not the wide-open beach, but a hut. She could sleep in a hammock. She wouldn't even care about the bugs. She'd sleep on the ground if she had to.

When they reach the car, Stewart helps Effie into the passenger seat, then gives Maeve a half-hug. "It's great to see you."

Maeve presses her head into his shoulder. "I can't do this," she says. He pats her head then hops cheerfully into the backseat with their mother and tells Maeve to giddy up.

24

It's a week after Maeve unwrapped the camera from Anita and Maeve has driven herself and her Cannon Sure Shot home from Anita's in her mother's Ford Escort. Maeve feels floaty with all she learned about contrast and lighting. She's thinking about the way Anita photographed sand by standing in the ocean and then on a rock, by sitting down, by bending over. She had Maeve hold the battery-operated spotlight they'd brought, but they'd also waited for the natural light to change from the filtered sun of early morning to the bright sun of afternoon. There were a few beachgoers, wrapped in scarves and hats and wool coats, who stopped and watched Anita with what Maeve thought was admiration.

Anita wore a long gray sweater, tight dark jeans, a scarf that looked like pearls stretched and flattened, and fluffy earmuffs the color of fog. Maeve resented the imperfectly knitted pink hat her mother made and which Maeve wore out of a sense obligation.

It's six o'clock and already pitch dark and Maeve is still thinking about Anita and so it takes her a moment to notice her mother sitting on the brick steps that lead up to their front door. "Hey," Maeve says, and then she realizes her mother is shivering.

She's annoyed by this. Annoyed that her mother has to ruin her good mood because she burnt the chicken or bacon or beef stew and is now outside because inside the house is filled with smoke. Maeve says, "Do you need me to go to the store?"

Her mother stands, adjusts her pale blue sweatpants. "I locked myself out of the house."

Her mother's nose and cheeks are very red.

"How long have you been out here?" Maeve fumbles her key into the lock.

"I thought your father would be home at five. I came out because I thought I heard his car and I wanted to tell him to park in the street because the plow guy hasn't come for the driveway yet." She shakes her head.

Her father had gone to the Haverlands' for drinks. Maeve left when he got there. When she saw her father in the hall, shrugging off his jacket, she'd said, "Charlie's not here."

Her father, laughing, said, "Anita knows where the liquor cabinet is."

Maeve took her time buttoning her coat, listening for evidence of his wrong-doing. Certainly, Effie wouldn't want him alone with Anita. Neither would Charlie, for that matter. There was always something flirty about the way her father and Anita were—something Maeve had only recently begun to realize. But now, when she thought back, it had always been there. The way they leaned into each other when they talked. The way they touched each other on the hands, arms, shoulders. They way they tracked one another with their eyes, all the time. Maeve rebuttoned two of the bottom buttons she'd mis-aligned. All she could hear was something about the taste of the new Haverland Health bars and Anita laughing and saying they should roll them in chocolate. Just work stuff. Still, it wasn't just work, was it? The tone of their voices. The soft edge of their laughter. The way Effie hated Anita.

And now, here was her mother outside in the cold.

"Couldn't you find the spare key?"

"It's under the porch," her mother says. Her socks are wool but she's not wearing shoes. "I didn't expect your father to be so late."

Maeve unlocks the door, holds it open so her mother can get in first.

In the warm hallway, her mother bends and rubs her toes. "Thanks for coming home," Effie says.

"Sorry I was late," Maeve says.

Effie says, "I called the Haverlands, hoping you were on your way. When Anita answered, I thought I heard your father in the background."

If Maeve acknowledges it was Tom, what will happen? Her mother might ask her father when he gets home, drunk and satisfied, what's going on. But he'll say "nothing." He'll say it was just business. He'll tell her there's nothing for her to worry about. She'll say she's not a fool. He'll say she's acting foolish. She'll ask why he does this to her and he'll say she's melodramatic. So, to spare them all, Maeve shakes her head. "Maybe it was Charlie."

Her mother smiles a tiny smile. "Charlie was on the news at five, just before I locked myself out, I saw him. He was doing a healthy cooking segment."

"Hm," Maeve says.

"You didn't see your Dad there? At the Haverlands'?"

"Anita and I were at the beach most of the day." Maeve is not a good liar, and as her heart ricochets around her chest, she reminds herself she's telling part of the truth.

Her mother nods, accepting or seeming to accept this half-truth.

"I'm hungry," Maeve says, even though she isn't. Anita had

put out a plate of brie and grapes and the expensive crackers Effie never buys. Maeve hadn't meant to eat as much as she had. And now she's not hungry, but she wants her mother to feel needed.

"I made beef stew," her mother says. "It might be a little burnt on the bottom, so scoop from the top."

*****

Later, her father is in the living room, feet up in his recliner, Hogan's Heroes on rerun, Captain and Coke in hand. Effie has gone to bed to get warm. Maeve stands in the doorway and watches until there's a commercial. "I told Mom I didn't see you at the Haverlands' tonight."

"Don't start on me, Maeve."

"So, I should have told her you were there even though Charlie wasn't?"

"Anita and I work together," he says. He clicks through a commercial for dog food.

"Mom was practically frozen when I got home." It's probably true that Anita and her father are just work-friends, because, really, what would Anita see in Tom? Charlie is taller and a much better dresser and he has money for a house on the lake and two BMWs, plus a truck. Maeve's father isn't short, but he's shorter than Charlie, and while he's objectively more handsome, he dresses like he shops at Kmart, because that's exactly where Effie buys his clothes. He's also charming, which is what Effie says is the thing that got her to fall for him in the first place. Sometimes she's says this like it's a good thing, and sometimes not.

"I've told her a thousand times to move the key to somewhere she can get at it." Hogan has returned and her father watches it as if he hasn't seen this very episode at least twenty times. It's the one where Hogan convinces Klink he's psychic.

"Maybe you could invite Ma to have drinks with you guys next time."

Her father flicks her a look. "Your mother has made it clear she doesn't want to spend time with Anita, and I'll start taking marital advice from you when you get a serious boyfriend, how's that?"

Heat rises in Maeve's cheeks. "This has nothing to do with me."

Her father turns back to the TV. "You got that right."

25

Maeve gives her mother a Twinkie and watches to make sure she sits up to eat it. She doesn't care that there will be crumbs in the bed. She'll change the sheets in the morning, which she now does most mornings because her mother has become incontinent at night and refuses to wear Depends.

When Maeve leaves her mother's room, she nearly trips over Paige who sits cross-legged in the hall.

"Are you okay?"

Paige has been crying. She looks up, and Maeve sees the streaks of both old and new tears. "Can you come in my room?" Paige asks.

Maeve has to pee and she's been holding it since she brought her mother the Twinkie, which was forty minutes ago. Maeve almost says she'll come later, but this will be the kind of thing Paige holds against her.

Paige's room is overheated and smells like corn chips and Maeve moves toward the window but Paige stops her. "Can you just listen?"

Maeve doesn't want to listen. She wants to pee and then sleep.

Paige sits heavily on her bed. "It's about me and Kris."

They broke up, Maeve thinks. Thank God. Also, this is something she can handle. She'll take Paige down to the kitchen and make chocolate chip cookies and eat most of the batter without cooking it and maybe Maeve will tell Paige about the first boy she ever loved—a boy with eyes the color of milk chocolate who dumped her for a girl who wasn't still wearing a training bra.

Maeve is so busy thinking about this that she almost misses the fact that Paige is clutching a pillow like it's a life raft on the Titanic. "I think he raped me," she says.

Maeve feels a laugh-bubble in the back of her throat and she has to swallow and swallow to get it to go down. No one "thinks" they got raped. There's date rape, but, still, Paige would know if she was date raped. Maeve has seen talk shows.

Maeve guesses Paige and Mohawk boy had sex and now Paige regrets it. Maeve wants to tell Paige women can't go around saying they were raped when they weren't because it makes other women who really were raped look bad. Some part of her is derailed by the pitiful look on Paige's face, though. Maeve feels hysterical with exhaustion and her need to pee.

"When?" This is the only concrete, semi-reasonable thing Maeve can come up with to say, but as soon as she says it, she can see it's not what Paige wanted her to ask. *I don't have time to be a better mother right now.*

Paige brushes her hair with her fingertips, brushes the legs of her knobby pink pajama pants, brushes her hands over the bedspread. She's barefoot and her toenails have recently been painted silver. "When you were at the doctor's with Gram. We went to his house because you said we couldn't be alone here," Paige says.

The accusation behind Paige's words make Maeve furious. Maeve has told her she's not allowed to be alone with Kris because she doesn't want her teenage daughter treating their house like a motel. What's so wrong about that? It doesn't mean she meant she could be alone with him at his house, and

Paige is smart enough to know that. Peter says they have to let her grow up sometime, that in a few years she'll go off to college, and that's all well and good, but they don't have to make it easy for her to have sex with a boy who was going to break her heart one way or another.

Maeve thinks about seeing Paige on her knees in front of Kris, both of them lit by the Christmas tree. She presses her fingertips into her eyelids and feels her heartbeat pounding in her eyes. Her bladder feels stretched to its limits and the tiniest trickle of pee starts to leak out.

"I can't do this right now." Maeve says. She's aware this makes her a terrible mother. It's possible you can only successfully be one thing at a time—mother, daughter, wife, employee, citizen.

"Mom—"

"No, Paige. No. You're fine. I'm fine. Everything is fine." Maeve isn't shouting or screaming, but her voice feels like fingernails on sunburnt skin. If she doesn't get to the bathroom soon, it's possible she'll wet her pants.

The fact something bad happened is exactly why they have rules about these things and Paige defying the rules is why she got herself raped. And, yes, Maeve feels bad for the how-can-you-be-my-mother look on Paige's face, but life isn't always fair. There goes another trickle of pee down her leg. In Paige's wicker trash basket is a white teddy bear wearing a Patriots t-shirt. His eyeballs have been plucked out.

Paige says, "I said no and he kept going."

Maeve clenches her teeth. "But you'd said yes before."

The teddy bear has stuffing coming out of where its legs should be.

Paige looks like she did when Maeve confirmed there

was no Santa Claus. That fucking know-it-all boy in her second-grade class told her and Paige begged to know the truth. Only the truth wasn't what she wanted, it turned out.

Paige says, "I can't believe you don't believe me."

There's a steady trickle down the inside of her leg now that will, in a matter of seconds, find its way to the pale strawberry-colored carpet Paige picked out when she was six.

Paige is looking down at her hands when Maeve kisses her lightly on the forehead. "You'll be okay," she says.

26

On the night of Maeve's work Christmas party, Flora has a cold and Natalie and Stewart have gone to the Nutcracker and so Maeve tells Peter they should stay home. But Peter says he wants to go. He likes talking to Dr. B about the charity Dr. B is involved with that helps kids with cleft palates.

Peter kisses the back of her neck and murmurs that it'll be nice for them to spend time together.

Paige says she'll "hang out" with her grandparents. She's barely spoken to Maeve since she told Maeve about the incident with Mohawk boy, and even now, she makes her offer to Peter. He probably thinks they're arguing about clothes or makeup, as usual.

Maeve has already unhooked the diamond earrings she borrowed from Collette and stepped out of her heels. Her desire to lie down is overwhelming.

"It'll only be for a few hours," Peter says.

It's been three days and Maeve hasn't told Peter about Paige and Kris. She thought Paige might tell him, but he wouldn't want to leave her if he thought she was in what he would certainly call a crisis. She should tell him, but the few times they've been alone and awake, she feels the words stick like lint on a sweater in her throat. She tells herself it's not an emergency. She tells herself she doesn't want to add to his worries. She tells herself it's possible Paige meant for her to keep it a secret.

Maeve has the odd sensation that, when she returns from the party, her parents and Paige will have pulled together a surprise party for her. She imagines herself pushing through a wall of balloons, blinking in the flash of a camera, thanking everyone for coming. She hasn't slept a full night since her mother moved in. And last night, she dreamt she was chasing Paige through a system of underground caves, all of them full of filthy, partially shredded teddy bears.

At the party, there's an abundance of red wine, even though Dr. B's house is a river of white carpet. She thinks of Anita Haverland's white living room and imagines her father sitting there with his Captain's and Coke.

Maeve drinks one glass of wine, and then another. She waves away the endive filled with shrimp salad, the little pancakes of something topped with something. She doesn't want food in her teeth and she likes the hollowness of her stomach, the way the wine pings her insides. It's not hard to understand what her father likes about drinking.

She texts Paige to see how things are going and Paige responds with a happy face emoji. Maeve texts back "Is Grandma asleep? Did she eat dinner? Did you lock the front and back doors?" More than twenty minutes later, Paige responds with a hang loose emoji. "Everything's fine," Paige texts, and Maeve has an urge to list all the things that aren't fine. *Anita Haverland. Your grandmother. You.*

Across the room, Peter leans against a white statue of a woman, talking to a woman who might be the statue's model about something that makes him wave his arms around. Maeve is on her third glass of wine and she's fighting the urge to lie down on the white white carpet and close her eyes. With considerable effort she waves. Peter doesn't see her.

And then Dr. B's wife is beside Maeve introducing her to Wendy-the-therapist who is Dr. B's wife's friend. Dr. B's wife obviously doesn't know that Maeve and Wendy have met in a professional capacity and Maeve is unsure of the protocol—is she supposed to laugh and admit she's been seeing Wendy as a therapist? Or should she pretend not to know her? If she says, "Oh, Wendy's my therapist" in that blithe way everyone says they have a therapist or a 401k, Maeve is afraid Wendy will ask her how Paige is. In their session yesterday, Maeve told Wendy about the rape but then she lied. She had meant to tell Wendy the truth, that she'd basically told Paige it was her own fault, but instead she told Wendy she'd assured Paige it wasn't her fault and said that rape is a kind of aggression and that no means no. Wendy had murmured assurances that she'd done exactly the right thing which confirmed to Maeve that Wendy was a crap therapist because she should have known Maeve was lying. Now, Maeve is afraid Wendy might ask about Paige in front of Peter, thinking he knows because Wendy suggested Maeve not keep secrets from her husband and Wendy is the kind of therapist who assumes people follow her advice.

Maeve shakes Wendy's hand and looks at her brooch, which is a quarter-sized Santa Claus face, topped with his signature hat, his expression more leering than jolly. Maeve smiles and asks Wendy what she does for a living. Wendy doesn't even blink, doesn't shake her head, doesn't smile in a knowing way. She says she's a therapist, just like anyone else would say "teacher" or "investment banker." Maybe she doesn't recognize Maeve with her eyeliner not smeared down her cheeks. Or, maybe she doesn't want Maeve to get all weepy and tell her how last night her mother bunched her hands in Collette's blond poof like it was cotton batting and asked how she got it like that. Then, while Collette laughed and held Effie's hands, Effie asked if it was a wig. Collette. Good Collette who later told Maeve that when she tried to gentle Effie's hands away from her hair, Effie shoved her so hard she nearly toppled off her stool. Collette had laughed, had said you wouldn't think a tiny woman could have so much strength. And Maeve laughed, too, even though she could feel herself drowning from the inside out. Maeve nods like "therapist" is the most interesting thing she's heard in ages.

She says, "Any crazy people lately?" She laughs a hard bark, and then she realizes she needs to pee.

She excuses herself from Wendy, even though Wendy has already turned away and is talking to Dr. B's wife about an art exhibit she saw recently in which someone made a fountain of red wine and had people made of grapes standing in it. Maeve picks her way up the white-carpeted stairs with her almost-empty glass of red. She finds a bathroom, pees, and then stares at herself over the sink while she washes her hands.

She does not look like her mother. Effie is round cheeked, with light brown hair gone silver. Maeve is angles and a high forehead, dark hair. She colored it last week, but already she can see the mean gray at her temples.

Attached to the bathroom is a bedroom, and Maeve sits on the white bedspread and drains her glass. It's probably not the master bedroom, because there's nothing on the dresser, nothing on the nightstand except a pile of books: "Man's Search for Meaning," "The Bell Jar," and "1001 Reasons to be Happy." Some people try so hard, Maeve thinks, but then the thought drifts away like a cloud before she can fully tease it out.

She feels pleasantly tired and water-logged, as if she's spent the day at the beach. She doesn't even know where she left her cell phone and she doesn't care, even though a part of her is aware she should care, because her mother could be dying and Paige would want to tell her that. She lies down, closes her eyes.

She thinks about Peter and the statue-woman and how the statue-woman probably doesn't have a mother with dementia, an alcoholic father, a delusionally optimistic brother, a daughter who thinks she's the worst mother in the world.

When she wakes, her mouth is cottony, and she checks the bed and the floor to make sure she hasn't thrown up.

Downstairs, everyone is where she left them, as if she's been gone no time at all. Peter is still in the living room, still talking to the statue-woman. He's relating the story about the therapy dog they just got for his classroom, a story through which Maeve nodded obligingly and through which this woman is dabbing glittery nails at black-lined lids because she is completely emotionally on board with Peter and his goodness. When Maeve touches his arm, he jumps, and she's grateful that he can feel her. She says, "Have you heard from Paige?"

He says, "I looked all over for you."

Maeve shakes her head, because of course he didn't.

The statue-woman touches Maeve's arm with her icy fingertips and says, "You're so lucky to be married to this guy."

"I lost my phone," Maeve says.

"Where did you lose it?"

Maeve turns to see if Wendy has heard this, because it's a ridiculous thing to say, and exactly the kind of thing Peter always says. It's the kind of things that makes her hate him, and even though her hate is temporary, Maeve worries it's also cumulative, like stains on a blouse.

Now she says, "Can I borrow your phone?" When he

hands it to her, she calls Paige and when Paige answers and says everything's fine, she hangs up without thanking her, calls back, says she loves her, then hangs up again and dials her own number, which she sees Peter has programmed under "Wife" and which bothers her because of its reductive nature.

Maeve wanders up the stairs, listening for her ringtone which she chose because it's called "dreamscape." Peter trails her. "Are you drunk?" he asks when she stumbles at the top of the stairs.

"Just tired," she says.

Her phone is on the bathroom sink and she retrieves it without even a glance in the mirror.

Peter says, "Did you hear from Paige?"

And Maeve, because she's drunk and sad, starts to cry.

"Hey," Peter says. He pulls her into him and she leans against his chest.

"She hates me," Maeve sobs.

He rubs her back in big, slow circles. "She's a teenager. She hates everyone."

"I should have been more sympathetic. I should have said we'd get her therapy or something. I don't know, Peter, what does anyone do with that kind of thing?" As soon as the words have tripped out of her mouth, the sober part of her brain realizes her mistake.

Peter stops rubbing her back. "What's happened?" He pulls away so he can see her face.

In the bathroom mirror, she and Peter are repeated back to her. They do not look happy.

"What's going on?" Peter asks.

"Nothing," Maeve says. "It's really nothing." They are so close Maeve can see a tiny smudge of shrimp cocktail sauce at the corner of Peter's mouth. "Paige came to me a few days ago and said something happened between her and Kris." Maeve would like to lean over and drink from the tap, but Peter's gaze won't let her move. "They had sex, which I'm pretty sure they've had before, but this time Paige said she didn't want to have sex and I guess Kris pressed her into it. She was pretty upset about the whole thing." This sounds almost reasonable to Maeve.

"Oh my god." Peter runs his hands through his hair. "Do you—it sounds like—Jesus—what did she say, exactly? Not, I mean—did he rape her?"

Maeve's face feels like it's been baked in a pizza oven. "That's—yes—that's what Paige said—"

"Oh my god." Peter has gone ashy. "That poor kid."

Maeve nods like that's exactly what she thought all along.

Peter paces. The bathroom is big as far as bathrooms go, but still, it's too small for his long strides. It's making Maeve dizzy. He says, "When did she tell you this?"

Maeve closes her eyes so she doesn't have to see her face in the mirror when she lies. "Yesterday?"

"I wish you'd told me. Why didn't you tell me as soon as she told you?"

"I've had a lot on my mind," Maeve says.

At this, Peter stops. "This is a really big deal, Maeve. You know that, right?"

Maeve waves a hand through the air, trying to wave away his anger, his upset. "I know, Peter, and she's fine. She's okay."

"Maeve, a violation like rape can cause lasting psychological damage."

Maeve shakes her head, even though this immediately seems like a bad idea because the bathroom begins to spin.

Maeve holds onto the sink. "I'm sorry, Peter, but you baby her. They'd had sex before—"

At that, he stops pacing. "No way, Maeve. No way you said that to Paige."

"Peter—"

"She's your daughter. She needs you."

Maeve can't stand her thirst anymore. She opens the cold water tap, dips her head, and takes a long drink. She rises and wipes her chin with her hand. "I'm not a bad mother."

Peter stares at her with disappointment. "I'm not sure Paige would agree."

"That's not nice."

She follows Peter out of the bathroom and down the stairs. He retrieves their coats and thanks Dr. B and his wife and even manages to tell the statue-woman it was nice to meet her. He has Maeve by the arm and they're out the door and into the car and on the way home before she can even say she's sorry. She's sorry for everything.

27

For years, Charlie Haverland and Tom traveled around the country offering presentation-slash-buffet dinners to promote Haverland Health. Charlie clicked through a slide show while Tom did most of the talking on the hazards of obesity and the benefits of Haverland Health products.

Even when pressed, they never revealed the price of their bars, smoothies, extracts, teas, and powders during the presentation. "It's worth it," her father would say, patting his trim waistline. "Trust me." Only during private consultations would price be discussed.

Once in people's homes, Tom and Charlie went through kitchen cabinets and refrigerators and freezers and deemed food "nutritionally void." They made a chart of the nutrients in Haverland Health foods. They made a graph of expected weight loss. They hardly ever left a house without a sale.

Maeve didn't see a presentation until her junior year of high school, when her friend Della's parents were going to one of the Haverland buffets. When they asked Maeve and Della to go, Maeve, who had zero interest in seeing her father act like a more insufferable version of himself, said she had a ton of studying to do, but Della wanted to go because there'd be free food and it would be weird to go without Maeve.

It was the week before Christmas. The hotel function room had tiny white lights on potted trees in each corner and at each end of the buffet table. The buffet table was set with stacks of plates and knives and forks rolled in red napkins.

Maeve's father straightened his microphone. He was wearing his Rudolph tie. The nose blinked red. "We'll eat at the break, folks." He smiled. His teeth gleamed in the light from the projector.

He drank from his water bottle. He asked how many people felt good—really good. "Really, really good," he said, drawing it out in a way that sounded sexual and made Maeve deeply uncomfortable. How many people could walk up a flight of stairs without losing their breath? Good. How about running a mile? Two miles? Few people raised their hands and Tom nodded gravely. He cited statistics about blood pressure, diabetes, kidney problems. He leaned closer to his microphone and said, low and conspiratorially, that he wanted to help each and every person in that room.

Her father made eye contact with everyone in the room, including Maeve. She looked down at her Nutrition Needs brochure so that he couldn't see how surprised she was. He was a different person in front of people—friendly, helpful, caring, even. It both impressed and bothered her.

And then Charlie dimmed the lights and Tom took a breath. "Here's why we're really here, folks." He rolled the video. A living room, a man and a woman on a worn green couch, both of them in blue plaid shirts. "We always just ate whatever we wanted, whenever we wanted," the man said. His wife smiled at him. A montage of them eating Oreos, Twizzlers, and giant sodas followed. In the montage, the couple was much heavier than the version of them on the couch, and Maeve found it unlikely they would have filmed themselves eating. It must be actors, or fat suits, or some other kind of trickery.

"Then, she got cancer."

"We didn't do nothin' but eat better," the woman said. "And, six months later..." she made a wavy motion with her hands, "No more cancer."

Maeve didn't believe a word of it, but Della's mother gasped her approval.

The film ended with a statistic about how many people die from obesity-related diseases every year. Her father took a long drink from his water bottle and told the twelve to help themselves to the buffet.

Della and her parents stood stiffly beside Maeve as they loaded their plates with salad dressed with Haverland Health vinegarette, chicken marinated in Haverland Health marinade, and carrots seasoned with Haverland Health Not-Salt. Haverland Health Healthier-Than-Water and Slimming Seltzer were the beverages on offer.

"It's amazing," Della's mother began, and then broke off to ask a server about salt and pepper. Pepper, she was told, was on the table. Salt was one of the things that was killing her.

Anita Haverland passed out samples of Haverland diet bars on a tray as if they were pieces of jewelry and this was the bidding portion of *The Price is Right*. She winked at Maeve as she passed and Maeve felt elevated, like she'd ascended to a platform, like she was more special than anyone else in the room. Anita's heels were very high, and her posture was perfect.

"You have to make the decision about what your life and the lives of your loved ones are worth," Charlie Haverland said as people drank their last sips of Haverland Tea. "We just want everyone to have all the information."

Della's parents agreed to have Maeve's father come to their house for a consultation. Maeve looked away while they filled out the paperwork, while they said mornings were better than evenings, while they agreed to both be there because, Charlie explained "it's a lifestyle change and it's so much better if everyone is on board."

Weeks later, Della got drunk at a party and told Maeve her father threw out nearly everything her parents had in their cabinets. He sold them three cases of bars and two of tea and, Della said, the cost was nearly as much as the leather jacket she'd been eyeing that her parents had said was too expensive. "He's good," Della said. "Your Dad. He scared the shit out of my parents. He's a very convincing liar."

Maeve flinched at that. It was one thing for her to think it, another thing entirely to hear it out loud from someone she genuinely liked.

Maeve walked Della home and held Della's hair off her face while she retched into the toilet. She said, "I don't know anything about my father's business." Because, while she could acknowledge he had some kind of charm, she also had a feeling Della's parents weren't the type to stick to a diet and that, in the end, they'd blame her father and Haverland Health, and possibly Maeve by extension. Della already was.

One night not long after, Maeve picked a fight with her father. She said, "You make money by inflating statistics and selling them a product that promises more than it can deliver."

Her father took a long drink. "If people use it correctly, it works," he said.

"You know that isn't true," Maeve said. Her legs felt like they contained a beehive. She did not try to stand, although she would have liked to go to her room.

"It's not my fault if people want to believe in something," her father said. And then he went into the living room and turned on the news.

Effie chopped a carrot into sticks she would keep in a glass of water in the fridge for a "sweet" snack. "You shouldn't talk to your father like that," she said.

What Maeve wanted to say was that it bothered her that he could make people believe things that weren't true, and also dis-believe things that were true, but for once she kept her mouth shut.

28

She could have stolen any one of the five Whitman Samplers brought to Dr. B's as hostess gifts. Or the plant, the hand towels, the cloth-bagged bottles of wine. Instead, Maeve heads to the mall with everyone else who was too late for even express shipping. Because she couldn't give Peter a Whitman's Sampler or Paige hand towels.

It should've made Maeve feel better that she wasn't the only one who still needed gifts on Christmas Eve, but it made her itchy and uneasy, as if she'd lost something. Which she had—her knack for organization, her ability to multi-task, her desire to please other people.

As soon as Maeve had her driver's license, which was the year she turned sixteen, her father gave Maeve money the week before Christmas—a hundred dollars, two hundred, it depended on his mood—and told her to get something for her mother. Maeve bought Effie fluffy sweaters in white and gray, Baby Soft perfume, drugstore sunglasses, a pearly pink bud vase, a thin gold bracelet with a clasp that broke when Maeve dug it out of her mother's jewelry box and tried it on, and which she put back, broken and confession-less. She bought her folk-art calendars and Willow Tree figurines and Denise Austin workout videos. She bought cards "To My Lovely Wife." She watched her mother's face for pleasure, but instead generally found suspicion and disappointment.

When Maeve left home for college, her father stopped

asking for her help. "We've given up on gifts," her mother said when Maeve asked what Tom gave her for her birthday. "Neither of us needs anything." Which Maeve supposed was better than getting things you didn't want, but it made her sad all the same.

Through the crush of the crowd, Maeve shoves her way straight to the purse store, which is at the opposite end of the mall from where she parked. By the time she gets there, she's sweating and the bright fluorescents make her sweat harder, so much so she can't even try to apply powder to her slick nose because it will clump up and make her look diseased. She wipes sweat from her eyes while she surveys the glass shelves lined with purse after purse. Nearly every purse is black and they are lined up like little leather soldiers. All she remembers about the purse Paige described is that it was black.

This afternoon, Stewart and Natalie are planning to make a gingerbread house with Effie and Paige and bring it to Tom at the Ever-yellow. Maeve's father has hardly left the house and yesterday, when she went over to get more of her mother's sweatpants and sweatshirts, he was sitting up in bed, a travel mug of Captain's in his hands, the two-liter bottle on his nightstand. Stewart says he's depressed, that Maeve should have a little empathy, that people can love more than one person at a time. She told him he's been in California too long.

At the purse store, a woman in a beige pantsuit wishes Maeve a "sincerely" Merry Christmas. Maeve could get Paige a gift card and let her come back and get whatever she wants. But Maeve has already imagined the moment when Paige opens the box (which Maeve will find the time to wrap), digs through the tissue paper, pulls up the exact purse she described and which she thought Maeve wasn't paying attention to. Her daughter will leap up and kiss Maeve and say she's the best mother in the world.

Only Maeve wasn't paying attention, and so she asks Sincerely Christmas what the most popular purse for a six-teen-year-old might be. Sincerely is all bright confidence as she leads Maeve to a boxy purse Maeve can't picture Paige liking. "Is there a second favorite?" Maeve asks.

But, no, Sincerely tells her this is The One.

The purse costs more than Maeve makes in a week, but she buys it anyway. Then she walks around the mall with it clutched to her chest, the plastic bag so hot against her skin she's afraid it might melt and leave a scar of plastic on the already ugly black purse.

She makes her way down the row of stores, choosing in one boutique a sweater with delicate gauzy butterflies lifting off the sleeves for her mother, in another a juicer for Stewart and Natalie, in the Dollar General a flashlight that spins and blinks for her father.

She's out of the mall, relieved, proud of herself, merging into traffic, calculating how much wrapping paper she has and wondering if she needs to stop at the Dollar Tree for more, when she realizes she didn't buy anything for Peter.

Last year, he bought her a string of pearls she hadn't even known she wanted until she had them around her neck and they felt like tiny weights. Every time she wears them, she feels held in place.

She stops at Cumberland Farms and buys fifty dollars' worth of scratch tickets and three Big Bite Reese's Peanut Butter Cups.

Last Christmas, her mother baked cakes for her, Peter, Stewart, and Natalie which she'd never done before. Since they became adults, she usually bought them sweatshirts or books or sets of striped sheets. Maeve and Peter exchanged glances as they unwrapped the tin foil, as they felt the brickness of the tiny Bundt cakes. They'd laughed at Effie and said she'd lost her baking touch. She shook her head, played along, said there must be something wrong with the oven. They should have known, but what good would knowing have done? It was only a month after that when Tom took her to the doctor's and called Maeve to say they were "pretty sure" Effie had stroke-related dementia.

Maeve doesn't stop for wrapping paper and, once home, she realizes there's just a sliver of green trees on a red background left on the roll. Not enough for anything. She could have had the purse gift wrapped at the store for "no additional charge" but she couldn't stand to stay there in those accusatory lights after she signed the credit card slip. In the end, she shoves everything into gift bags, most of them birthday bags, although she makes panels out of the Christmas paper and tapes them over the frogs and ducks wearing party hats.

*****

On Christmas morning, Peter wins two dollars on one scratch ticket, nothing on any of the others. He scratches each ticket with so much enthusiasm, Maeve thinks he's joking.

"I didn't know what to get you," she says.

Peter uses the side of a quarter to reveal a seven. "This is excellent," he says. Sometimes his niceness feels aggressive. She told him she'd talk to Paige about what happened with Kris. She promised to get her into therapy. She knows he's trying to forgive her and that, for now, he's pretending he already has.

Effie picks a butterfly off her sweater and holds it in her

palm as if she believes it's real.

Stewart and Natalie insist they love the juicer. Maeve guesses they already have one—after all, they live in California and extol the virtues of kale. She should have bought them something else, or asked if they already had a juicer, or known they already had a juicer. Fleetingly, Maeve thinks about giving them Effie, of putting a ribbon loosely around her mother's neck and shouting "Happy Holidays!" So that she doesn't offend Natalie, who apparently considers herself some kind of Mother-Earth-slash-Buddhist.

Maeve hands Paige the purse, which she ended up squeezing into a Snoopy Valentine's Day gift bag because it was the only one she could find in her box of used gift bags that would fit the purse. She has taped a panel of Christmas tree wrapping paper over Snoopy's heart balloon.

Paige says, "Thank you" in the polite way Peter and Maeve have taught her. She re-wraps the purse in its pink tissue paper.

Maeve looks at her face, the fallen-in look of someone who did not get what they wanted, and feels an intense desire to hit her daughter, which scares her enough to make her stand up and ask if anyone wants coffee.

Paige's purse has a thin strap of interlocking gold rings. Now that Maeve has seen it in the lap of her sixteen-year-old daughter, she can tell it's an old lady purse.

When Maeve was a teenager and would tell her mother to leave her alone or mind her own business, Effie would sometimes chase her up the stairs and into Maeve's bedroom and around the bed and Maeve would hold up her hands and Effie would slap them away and Maeve would say sorry sorry sorry. And then Effie would call Maeve ungrateful and she'd storm out and Maeve would cry. Later, they'd meet in the kitchen and carve cheese from a block and eat it with apple slices and pretend nothing happened.

There's a light on in the bedroom, and when Maeve goes to shut it off, she finds Effie on the bed, the sweater cut in half. Maeve reaches for her mother's hand but Effie slaps her away.

"What are you doing, Ma?"

"He probably got this from that woman. He thinks I'm stupid."

Maeve's heart stutters. She steps closer but this time doesn't touch her mother. "I bought you that sweater, Ma." She wonders if she should tell Effie that Anita is dead, but what if Effie says she's glad?

"You always loved her more than you love me." Effie is crying now, great gulps of childish tears, and Maeve worries this will somehow cause another stroke. She wants to call to Stewart, who's mere presence seems to put her mother in an almost euphoric mood, but she can't take the chance that this one time her mother won't recognize him, that she'll think he's a stranger, that she'll get more upset.

"I'm sorry you don't like the sweater." Maeve's trying to be kind, but she can hear the edge to her voice, the bitter disappointment of disappointing her mother. There's no point in trying to stop her mother now—the sweater can't be saved.

"He bought me that nail polish—I don't wear nail polish and he knows it—and now this. This was probably one of *her* sweaters. It's exactly the kind of thing she wears." Effie pulls at a thread until it puddles in her lap.

Is it the kind of thing Anita would have worn? Is that why Maeve wanted it?

Finally, the sweater is just yarn and Effie stops. Maeve kneels, gathers the yarn into a pile, and carries it to the trash.

29

Stewart says their father "adored" the gingerbread house.

"Adored?" Maeve asks. She's put the kettle on for tea, but Stewart says he just wants hot water.

"It's better for your digestion."

Maeve dunks her teabag extra long and adds more honey than usual, just to show her brother how extravagant she can be.

They're at the kitchen table, watching snow slide off the roof. Maeve says, "How does Dad seem to you?"

"Depressed. But who wouldn't be? He was with Anita for what? Thirty years?"

Maeve flinches at the way Stewart says this so casually, especially when Effie might wander into the kitchen at any moment. "I guess," she says.

Stewart stirs his hot water nonsensically. "That's a real commitment."

"You say that like it's a good thing." Effie has gone to her room to nap, Peter, Paige, and Natalie have gone to the movies. Maeve can't remember which one but it doesn't matter.

Stewart shrugs. "I don't know if it's good or bad, but it's dedication, for sure."

They sit in silence, listening to the thwmping of the snow as it lands on piles of older, crustier snow. After a while, Maeve says, "There's a part of me that's relieved she's dead."

Stewart blows on his hot water, then sips. "You don't mean

that."

"What would have happened if she'd told her version of what happened? What if the police came and interrogated Mom?" Maeve didn't even feel the warning of tears before they come, a furious waterfall from her eyes and nose.

Effie is in her bedroom, singing the Chickadee song.

Stewart leaves his mug and wraps his arms around Maeve and she leans into him. His bags are packed. He says, "Shhh. I don't know what would have happened, honey, but it didn't happen. Everything's okay."

Maeve sniffles. "Nothing's okay." She feels like a little girl, but she doesn't hate the feeling of being comforted by her big brother. "What if we're letting her get away with murder?"

"We're not."

Stewart is still holding her, and Maeve's neck is starting to kink, but she doesn't want him to let go. Their plane leaves tonight.

He says, "It was probably an accident, Maeve. Whatever happened. It probably wasn't intentional and I don't know what good it would be to have Mom—or Dad for that matter—face charges."

Maeve tenses. "I don't get why Anita would say Mom pushed her if she didn't."

Stewart's laugh is a rumble against Maeve's cheek. "It's not like they liked each other."

"You're going to leave and go home to your kale salad and coconut water and your regular life and you won't have to deal with any of this."

"I know. I'm sorry."

He doesn't sound sorry and Maeve almost tells him he should stay, that they're his parents, too, that it isn't fair that she's stuck with them. But what good would that do? Natalie wouldn't stay in Maine forever and Stewart wouldn't leave her. If Maeve tells him to stay, he'll tell her he can't and she won't be able to forgive him and then she'll have one fewer person anchoring her to this life.

"I'll do whatever I can from California," he says.

She's glad he can't see her face because she's sure she looks anything but grateful. There's nothing he'll be able to do from California, and they both know it.

"I know you will," she says.

30

Paige has gotten a job at the Parker Cinemagic, which has been remodeled since Maeve and Stewart's teenage years with fresh carpet and paint along with reclining seats. The concession stand hasn't changed, though, other than that they now offer hot dogs along with the popcorn and Twizzlers and soda. Most nights, Peter picks her up and Maeve assumes he hears about whatever there is to hear about—the guy who always wants two soda flavors mixed, the kid who threw up in the lobby, the teenagers she caught sneaking into a second movie at the end of the first. Alongside deeper conversations about how Paige is feeling and doing and what's on her mind. Even when Maeve remembers to ask how work was, Paige just says "fine." Maeve knows she isn't asking the right questions, isn't trying hard enough.

Tonight, Peter has a charity bowling event and so Maeve is the one to pick up Paige. Her shift ends at 6:30. Maeve, in a flash of inspiration, suggested they see the 6:45 showing of "Little Women." Before Effie moved in, Maeve and Paige went to the movies every other week. They saw romantic comedies, mostly. They ate popcorn and M&Ms and drank Diet Coke.

"I heard it's really good," she texted. Paige texted back a smiley face emoji which Maeve took as enthusiastic agreement.

At 6:00, Maeve and Effie are playing Rummy. Effie has all her cards face-up and has demanded Maeve do the same. This on-display version of Rummy started a few weeks ago, and at first, Maeve laughed, assuming Effie was joking because how can you play cards if all the players know each other's hand? But Effie was serious to the point of tears, and so, Maeve turned her cards over and has been turning them over ever since.

Maeve plays her last run of three threes, puts on jeans, a light sweater, low boots, and lip gloss. She brushes her teeth and hair. She feels a flutter like getting away with something.

On the way out, she tells Collette she'll have her phone on if she needs her.

"We'll be fine," she says. She's taken Maeve's seat and is dealing the next hand of face-up Rummy. Maeve was embarrassed to have to ask Collette to come over, but she can't trust her father to be sober, which she didn't tell Collette, but she probably doesn't have to. She said he wasn't feeling well and Collette accepted that like she accepts everything—this face-up version of Rummy, Effie's teeth in the glass beside her—with unflappable cheer.

Maeve sits in her car at the Parker Cinemagic. She wants to be on-time, right at the end of Paige's shift, but not early enough to embarrass Paige. She texts Paige: "Here!" She adds and then deletes a smiley-face emoji. She's shaking a little, like she's cold, only she's not cold because she has her heat blowing pleasantly on her face. And her breath feels hitchy, as if she's nervous, which is silly because she's here to see a movie with her daughter.

She read *Little Women* to Paige when she was eight, and then they read it together when Paige was twelve. This will be fun. This will be great.

Maeve texts Stewart to make sure everything's okay and to

remind him there's a tuna noodle casserole ready to go in the oven. "Three-fifty for forty-five minutes," she says.

At 6:20, Maeve goes in. Paige is behind the counter, scooping popcorn into a large bucket. Maeve smiles, but her stomach feels turned inside out. She tries to take a deep, calming breath, but it hitches again and then she wonders when the last time she took a deep breath was and then she tries to force it and she can't get a breath at all and then she starts to panic that she's not breathing. She knows she's still breathing because she's standing upright, but she doesn't feel like she's getting enough air into her lungs. "I'll get the tickets," Maeve manages to say when Paige meets her gaze. She can't believe Paige hasn't asked her what's wrong because she must look like she's about to collapse. She really needs to sit down. She can go to the restroom as soon as she has the tickets.

"Got 'em," Paige says. "Go ahead in and I'll be right there."

Thank god. Maeve shuffles down the navy hallway, all of it too dark and too close and fuzzy. Why are the walls fuzzy? She reaches out to touch them, to make sure she isn't hallucinating fuzziness, and then yanks her hand back because they really are fuzzy. How has she never noticed that before?

She uses the restroom and washes her hands with a feeling of being very small inside her body, like a mouse in a maze only the maze is her liver and pancreas and kidneys and stomach.

She finds a seat and sits and tries to take normal breaths, despite what now feels like several mice trying to find their way out of her body. The previews are playing by the time Paige finds her.

They each have their own popcorn, Paige's with butter and Maeve's without, and their own Diet Coke. Maeve can feel the heat from Paige's arm, smell the strawberry lip gloss she's rubbed on. This is good, she thinks. This is good this is good this is good.

Maeve says, "Have the walls always been fuzzy?"

"Helps keep the sound down," Paige says.

Maeve laughs a little ha ha ha. She feels each "ha" like a pop in the back of her throat.

She forgot to tell Collette to take the Saran off the tuna noodle casserole, but she knows that, doesn't she? Maeve could text her, if she shields her phone so it doesn't bother anyone because she's not a rude moviegoer, but what if Collette doesn't hear her text alert, which is some kind of bird? She could go into the lobby and call her. It would only take a minute.

"I just need to make a quick call," she whispers to Paige. But, when she tries to stand, both her back and chest feel as though they're being grabbed by giant claws. The mice have grown. She can't take a single step. The people behind her hiss at her to sit down, and so she does.

Collette won't serve Effie a casserole that has melted Saran on it. She won't. She won't mistake it for cheese or not see it at all because it's clear. The whole point is that it's clear plastic. She should start to buy the tinted Saran—she's seen it and blue and pink but it's more expensive and what is it even for except for people like her parents who might eat the clear Saran?

Now she feels as though the "ha" has caught in her throat. She swallows, but it will not pop. It's lodged there and she can't swallow. She can't swallow, but she must be swallowing around the "ha."

Maeve hasn't remembered tissues, but she grabbed a handful of napkins and she pulls them from her jacket pocket and hands some to Paige. Paige smiles at her and takes the napkins and Maeve feels pleasure at her motherliness. What made her think to hand Paige the napkins? She can't remember. Has she had a stroke? Is she having a stroke?

Was it possible Anita Haverland had a stroke and fell down the stairs? Or maybe it was really like Tom said and she was just startled by Effie and fell and she said what she said to Maeve to be cruel. Maybe the brain injury made her cruel. Or maybe she was always cruel. Oh, god, their friendship must have hurt Effie terribly and what kind of person is Maeve? And now she's dead. Maeve can't believe Anita is dead and that she never got to tell her how much she meant to her and how sorry she was that their friendship ended so badly.

No, not sorry. She should not be sorry.

Yesterday, Effie thought Paige was Grace and kept asking her how she was feeling and what she'd done with her hair.

Maeve will sit here and breathe and give it five minutes and if she still thinks she's having a stroke, she'll go into the lobby and have someone call Peter to come and get her. There's a man screaming on screen and Maeve whispers, "We're in the wrong theatre."

"It's the trailer," Paige whispers back. She smiles at Maeve, like it isn't weird at all that Maeve didn't realize this.

Maeve can't settle. The mice tug unpleasantly, no matter which way she sits. And the popcorn hasn't landed right in her stomach. It feels like it's still popping. She sips her soda, which only makes her stomach more unsettled.

One year on Halloween, her father had the idea—or maybe Stewart had the idea and talked her father into it—of having a bonfire. "People do it all the time," Stewart said to Maeve, who was wearing a highly flammable Peter Pan costume her mother had purchased for her at Walgreens. They had the bonfire and Stewart and his friends listened to Ratt and Quiet Riot and tossed empty soda cans into the flames to watch them snap and disintegrate while Maeve stayed along the fringes, the fear of bursting into flames crawling all over her that night.

And now, here in the dark with Jo and Meg and Amy and poor, doomed Beth on the screen, Maeve feels the same terror. "Help," she says to Wendy-in-her-head. Wendy tells her to try the breathing they practiced in her last session. But Maeve's breaths flutter somewhere just below her ribcage, trapped by her underwire bra. She reaches back, pretends to scratch, and unhooks her bra.

Still, she can't breathe and now her bra cups are loose and she feels untethered and she'll never be able to re-hook it without reaching up under her shirt, which she'll have to do in the bathroom.

Are shallow breaths enough to sustain a person? She's still alive, so she's fine. She's fine. Wendy nods at this.

And then, Maeve can't see Wendy anymore. She can't see the March sisters on screen, either. She can't see anything and she thinks it's either because she has her eyes closed or that she's gone blind. Her heart is beating as if she's just run up the stairs with a full basket of laundry.

Maeve tries to be as still as possible. She tries to keep her eyes pointed in the direction of the screen, which is where she assumes the movie is still playing. She tries to put a smile on her face.

Paige says, "Are you all right?"

There's a pain like she's being stabbed from the inside of her ribcage out. Maybe there's a mouse with a pickaxe in there. Also, she can see now—the bright blur of the screen, the nubby red of the seatback in front of her. Maeve wants to say yes, she's fine, I'm fine, honey, can I have a chocolate? Is that what they're called? The word sounds funny in her head: chalk-late. She says it a few more times.

But she's not fine, and it will be much worse, much more damaging for Paige later in life, if it turns out this is when Maeve dies, and so Maeve says, "I think I might need some help."

Maeve, hunched into herself like a woman faking a heart attack, semi-stands. Paige, sweet Paige, stands and loops an arm around her back. "Mom?" Paige whispers. She isn't the kind of daughter who would like Anita Haverland more than she likes her own mother. Who can't believe Anita is dead and her mother, who ate Ajax with her breakfast, is alive.

"I think I'm okay," Maeve says.

They inch forward, one step every hundred years, until they're in the lobby.

Paige signals to the manager. She's so competent and she still has on her black pants and Cinemagic shirt. She's a good kid. Maeve doesn't want to die right here. Maeve thinks Paige says, "My Mom is sick."

The manager, who isn't much older than Paige, leads Maeve to a bench next to the claw game and Maeve rests her head on the cold metal and thinks he's a very nice young man.

Paige, beside her, rubs Maeve's arm, which Maeve would like her to stop doing, but which she won't say, even if she could manage enough strength to talk.

When the ambulance arrives, the paramedics give her a paper bag to breathe into and Maeve would laugh if she could laugh because she thought the breathing in a bag thing was only on TV. She breathes and they hook her up to some machines and say they'd like to take her to the hospital, to make sure it isn't a heart attack, even though they think it's just a panic attack. The way they say "just a panic attack" makes Maeve feel foolish, like a heart attack would at least not be a waste of everyone's time.

The pain has lessened to more of a pinch than a pickaxe. She says, "I'm only forty-nine."

The EMTs nod.

Paige says, "You should go, Ma."

"I can't leave you here."

"I'll call Dad."

Maeve refuses the stretcher and walks herself into the ambulance. Everyone watches her like she might explode.

*****

It's not a heart attack. She's treated and released that same night. Peter and Paige get to the hospital while Maeve is being examined by the bland ER doctor and Peter holds her hand and tells her she's going to be fine.

In the car, Peter tells her he loves her.

. The doctor said Maeve's "event" was a panic attack. He prescribed an anti-anxiety medication, which Wendy suggested a month ago. "I'll take the pills," Maeve says now, to appease Peter.

Peter squeezes her hand. He's quiet as they round the corner onto Acorn. Finally, he says, "You scared us tonight."

"I scared myself."

31

Two weeks after Maeve's sixteenth Christmas, Effie has made pasta with meatballs and it's ready, the pasta overcooking in the sauce, all of it being kept warm on the stove.

It's been forty-five minutes since Effie drained the pasta, anticipating Tom's imminent arrival. She's wiping down the insides of the microwave with a fistful of paper towels.

"He's probably stuck in traffic," Maeve says.

"He was having drinks with the Haverlands'," Effie says. Her mouth has the fine lines of a former smoker, the kind that remind Maeve of a cupcake liner, although she's only ever seen her mother smoke occasionally with Aunt Grace or Collette.

She scrubs at stuck on sauce or butter so hard the whole microwave shakes and Maeve worries it will crash to the floor. She crosses the room and puts her hands on either side of it to steady it.

"You're in my way," Effie says. And then, "I'm sure he knows better than to drive if he's had too much to drink." But it's clear from the way she says it that she's worried.

Maeve puts on her boots and Effie says she'll call the Haverlands' again. Her mother hates to drive at night. She says the oncoming lights look like strobe lights and Maeve says she should get her eyes checked and Effie insists it's just the way her eyes are, that she can get by. Once, she drove them up onto the library's lawn because she misjudged a left turn.

Maeve has had her license for eleven days, but still the

drive to the Haverlands' feels familiar. She pulls down the long, twisty driveway the Haverlands' have lined with wooden posts and twinkling white lights. It's on the verge of what her mother would call tacky, but Maeve loves the way it looks like something out of a fairy tale. They'll leave their Christmas lights up until February, because, Anita says, winter is too bleak without them.

Maeve thought they knew she was coming, that Effie would have called and said she was coming, but maybe there was no answer. There aren't any lights on as she approaches the house, even after she gets out of the car and slams the door.

It's only when she's on the porch, when she has her finger on the bell but not yet pressing, that she sees them—her father and Anita Haverland way in the corner of the living room. They're standing in front of the fireplace, their backs toward Maeve, but she can see the tension in their bodies. Maeve wouldn't be able to say how she knows, exactly, but it's something in their posture, something in the way they're angled away from each another, that suggests they're arguing. She wants to tap on the window to let them know she's there and also to stop whatever argument might be happening. The phrase that springs to her mind is "lovers' quarrel." She also wants to see what happens.

There's no doubt it's her father and Anita Haverland. Maeve's father is much shorter and stockier than Charlie Haverland. Plus, he's wearing a baseball cap and Maeve has never seen Charlie cover up his head of silver hair. And it's Anita's distinctive pouf of yellow hair, crinkly from hair spray and a curling iron, next to him. It could be some other man with Anita Haverland, some other man who has not yet come home for dinner, some other man who was supposed to be at this house for drinks and who hasn't left. But he turns his face to say something sharp and it's Maeve's father.

Maeve stands there for a long time. There's a fire going in the fireplace, and two wine glasses, half full of dark liquid. Her father occasionally drinks something other than rum and Coke, but not often. Everything about the scene says it's meant to be romantic.

They move close enough to kiss, then apart again. Their arms split the air between them. Anita's face, from what Maeve can see, is pulled by fury.

Anita Haverland, when they were all last there for dinner, made a big thing about how she's afraid she'll burn her eyebrows off if she tries to get a fire going. Her father is good at fire, making them in their backyard firepit almost every night in the summer so that Maeve and Stewart can toast marshmallows.

Tom arches back and Maeve thinks he's going to storm off and she prepares to duck below the window, but instead he lunges forward, arms outstretched, and shoves Anita. She stumbles, catches her foot on the rug, and falls into the leather armchair beside the fire. Her face has gone slack with surprise. Maeve feels sick. She should run back to her car. She should go home. Tom stands over Anita now, yelling, and her beautiful throat is tipped up and she's yelling right back at him. Maeve begins to shake. It's the kind of tremble that begins at the bones and moves outward, like an earthquake. They look like they could kill each other. They also look, confusingly, like they're in love.

In a kind of blind panic, Maeve finds a rock as big as her fist and carries it back to the car with her. She stands at her door, car running, door open. She lobs the rock at the house as hard as she can. She's only ten feet from the back of the house, but she throws the rock with all her force. She's aiming for the garage door because she thinks the sound of the impact will make her father and Anita go outside to investigate, that once the spell is broken, her father will come home and none of this will have happened.

Instead, she hits one of the five windows that sit above the garage door. The second from the far left. She hits it hard enough that it shatters, that the rock goes through and lands with a great clank onto whatever is on the other side.

Maeve has never played sports other than in gym class, and yet it turns out she might have been a good pitcher.

She flings herself into her car and, without buckling her seatbelt, wrenches her car around and drives away as fast as she can. She feels the tug of the edge of the driveway and she knows she should slow down, that sliding off into the woods on either side will mean she has to explain herself to Anita and her father. The porch light goes on and Anita and Tom appear as shadows. She knows they've seen her, but she's seen them, too. She makes it onto the road and presses the gas as hard as she dares.

When she gets home, she tells her mother she rang the Haverlands' bell but no one came to the door.

"They must have been in the basement," Effie says. The Haverlands' have a finished basement with black indoor/outdoor carpet and a gleaming black bar.

Effie has put out a bowl of pasta for Maeve. She has covered it with Saran wrap that has become wet with condensation.

When her father gets home, he says the Haverlands' invited him to stay for dinner. He says he tried to call, but that he got a busy signal. Effie says she must have forgotten to hang the phone up. Maeve says nothing.

32

Maeve is about to call Dr. B's patients for Monday when she picks up the phone and Peter is on the line. She almost hangs up because she doesn't have the emotional bandwidth to deal with him telling her he has a charity bowling event or night at the soup kitchen or save the kittens' campaign. Then he says hello in a way that seems almost desperate.

"Hi," she says. "Hey."

He laughs a little, like he's relieved he has the right place, the right person. And then he says, "I just wanted to remind you about the cake." He's been gentle with her since the panic attack, as if her weakness undoes all the ways she's failing as a mother and a wife.

Still, she hates the way he says this as though he's keeping her from embarrassing herself because he knows full well she has or will forget. The fact is, she doesn't remember anything about a cake. It's not his birthday, or Paige's. She tries hard to think of what else it might be but all she can come up with is New Year's Eve but that's not until Monday.

"What're we celebrating?" She asks in what she hopes is a semi-joking way. She digs through her purse and searches the yellow post-it notes she's taken to sticking on her license and sure enough, there's one at the top that says cake, huge exclamation point finishing off the word. Seeing it doesn't help her remember.

Peter laughs, then stops laughing. She hears a door open

and the whoosh of air as he steps outside. "Paige took her driving test today."

Maeve smiles hard at Irene as she leads the next patient in. Maeve says, "I didn't forget." She did, and she knows Peter knows. At least she found Paige a therapist. Peter took her to her first appointment yesterday and said it went well. Maeve wanted to ask more, but she didn't know exactly what to ask, and then her mother came into the kitchen to put the kettle on and Maeve took over making her tea so she wouldn't set the kitchen on fire.

Peter says, "Can you see if Dairy Queen has something with a car on it?"

"Yes, of course." The second line begins to ring and Maeve asks Peter to hang on while she gets it. The other call is a woman who has just broken a tooth and, before Maeve can get her scheduled, she wants to tell Maeve all about how it happened (eating a French fry, of all things). Finally, Maeve gets back to Peter in time to hear him say to Paige, "Mom. She'll be home soon with a surprise."

"The thing is," Maeve says. "I have to take my mother to a doctor's appointment this afternoon."

"Can't your father do that?"

Maeve hesitates. "I don't know." Without risking being overheard by Dr. B or Irene, she can't say he's hardly ever sober these days and she doesn't want him driving her mother anywhere—or driving, period. She says, "I should be home by six, though."

"Paige wants to meet at Applebee's. You can bring your Mom and meet us there." Peter sounds determinedly optimistic.

Maeve doesn't know how Effie will be after the appointment. Tired, confused, possibly angry. Dinner at a bright, loud, and unfamiliar restaurant is probably a terrible idea. "Sounds good," she says. "I'll call when we're done at the doctor's."

"I can get the cake," Peter says.

Maeve says no, that's okay, she'll do it. She'll get just the right cake and they'll all sing "Happy License" to the tune of "Happy Birthday." She'll get candles, too.

*****

It's closer to six-thirty when they get to the restaurant because one, Maeve couldn't find a parking spot at the doctor's office and two, Maeve couldn't find the car when it was time to leave. In the parking lot, her mother shuffled along beside Maeve, pointed to almost every car, and asked, "Is it this one? What did you say it looked like again?" And to top it all off, the parking lot was icy and all Maeve could picture was her mother falling and breaking a hip. Or sliding under the car and languishing there, trapped, Maeve unable to reach her, Maeve forced to call the fire department to rescue her mother and then never getting to the restaurant.

When they finally stopped at Dairy Queen, her mother said she'd wait in the car and Maeve said she needed her help picking out the cake. Effie said she was tired and Maeve promised it would only take five minutes but Effie flatly refused to get out of the car. And so, Maeve picked the first car design she found in the book and asked the girl to write "Congratulations, Paige!" She kept looking out the window, kept her finger on the door lock on her key fob, and paid for the cake without looking at it.

Finally, they get to the restaurant and Maeve has to beg her mother to get out of the car. "Why are you doing this to me?" Effie asks.

It's too cold and no way can Maeve keep the keys in the car with it running with her mother in it. She says, "There are people you know in here." When her mother seems unmoved by this, Maeve adds, "And hot chocolate." She doesn't like treating her mother like she's a child, but what choice does she have?

Her mother sighs and unbuckles her seatbelt.

At first Maeve doesn't see them through the throng of people. Waitresses dash around tables. Kids slide from chair to floor. Crayons are handed over and thrown. Beside her, Effie says, "What kind of place is this?" Finally, Maeve spots Peter waving at her and then she sees Paige, head down as if she's been crying, which means she probably didn't get her license and Maeve will be driving her around for eternity. Wendy-in-her-head raises an eyebrow. Fine, Maeve amends, not eternity. Just until she takes the test again. Whenever that will be.

They've already ordered appetizers, which are piled in front of them, and by the time Maeve and Effie have crossed the room, Paige has raised her head, mozzarella stick in hand, and is telling Peter about how the driving instructor had her back down the street "like a hundred feet."

Maeve blows a kiss to Peter and pulls out a chair for her mother. She kisses Paige on the cheek. "Congratulations," she says, hopefully.

Paige smiles. Thank god. Her mother reaches for her menu with one hand, a jalapeño popper with the other.

"You don't like spicy food," Maeve says, but Effie already has the popper in her mouth. She chews it once, twice, and then spits it into her palm. Maeve napkins the chewed popper off her mother's hand, not looking at Peter or Paige.

"I think I'll have the chicken," Effie says, handing Maeve

her menu.

There are at least twelve chicken entrees, but Maeve decides it'll be easier to make an educated guess and pick one her mother will like rather than ask her to clarify.

Peter orders steak and Maeve gets a cup of French onion soup, hold the cheese, and the fish tacos, and Paige orders shrimp alfredo. Maeve wonders if her mother will comment on Paige's fattening choice, but her mother is eating the spinach-artichoke dip with her fingers. Maeve pretends not to notice and Peter and Paige either really don't notice or don't care. If they don't care, Maeve is simultaneously grateful for their easy-going natures and dismayed by their lack of sanitary concerns.

After they order, they stare awkwardly at each other while Effie licks her fingers. Maeve sips her water every few seconds so she'll have something to do. "The test was easy?" She asks finally.

"Because if it wasn't easy, I couldn't have passed?" Paige snaps.

Maeve looks at Peter for backup, but he's wiping dip off Effie's hands. "That's not what I meant," Maeve says. "Don't talk to me that way, Paige."

Peter looks up and Maeve half-expects him to chide her here in front of everyone, remind her that Paige has been through "trauma" and that she needs time to "heal." He smiles at Maeve. "Paige, tell your Mom how far you had to back up."

"It was a mile, at least," Paige says, but without the same enthusiasm Maeve's heard her use when she told Peter.

"That's impressive," Maeve says. *See how normal we are?* Maeve thinks. *See how great this is? No trauma here!*

When the food comes, Effie pushes her chicken parmesan away. "That's not what I ordered," she says.

"It looks great," Maeve says with as much cheer as she can muster. She cuts the chicken up for her mother and repositions the plate.

"No," Effie shakes her head when Maeve offers her a bite. She points to Paige's plate. "That girl has what I ordered."

Paige hovers mid-bite.

"That's not what I ordered," Effie tells the waiter, who leans in to see what the problem is.

"It's fine," Maeve says. "Do you want my tacos instead?"

"I want what I ordered," Effie says.

Paige says, "What did you order, Gram?"

"This is what she ordered," Maeve says.

"That," Effie says, pointing to Paige's alfredo.

Maeve shakes her head. "That much milk will make you gassy."

"Geez, Mom, she's not a little kid."

"I'm the one who'll have to deal with her upset stomach later."

"Don't talk about her like she isn't even here. You always deny things as if that makes anything better." Paige moves her plate in front of Effie and takes Effie's plate to her. "Let's trade, Gram. The waiter must have screwed it up."

Maeve checks to see if the waiter has overheard this because she doesn't want him to think they think this is true, but he has wisely moved on to a less problematic table of two old women in matching sweatshirts eating tomato soup. Maeve doesn't deny that she denies things because that will, of course, prove Paige's point.

Effie beams at her. "You're a nice girl." And then she eats

the entire plate of shrimp alfredo.

Maeve should thank her daughter, tell her she's thoughtful, offer to share her fish tacos with her. But she's too dismayed to think clearly. Who are these people? How is she supposed to know how to behave when they keep changing all the rules?

Maeve wipes the drippy mess from her tacos off her hands and scoots out to the car for the cake. It's only as she pulls it out of the bag that she finally looks at it, finally sees that it reads: "Congratulations, Page." The car is a dopey cartoon character. She'd like to cry. She'd like to sit on the snowy, frozen tar and weep for all the things she's not getting right. But she doesn't have the luxury of that kind of self-mortification.

Maeve un-tapes the edges of the plastic dome and, with the nail of her pinky finger, scratches an "i" between the a and g. She forgot candles, otherwise she could stuff one right there and maybe no one would notice the missing "i."

She walks in with it, smiling, smiling. "Congratulations, honey!" She places the cake in front of Paige, but facing Peter, as if that will make it so Paige doesn't notice.

Effie stands and sways a bit.

"Are you feeling all right, Ma?"

"Oh, yes." She's scanning the room.

"Do you need the bathroom?"

She has her by the arm and they're moving, nearly halfway across the room, when Effie bends forward and vomits up all of the alfredo. "Oh, God," Maeve says. She does not look at Peter and Paige.

The hostess materializes with a mop and bucket in a matter of seconds and Maeve tells herself this kind of thing must happen all the time. Or, maybe not *all* the time, but often enough that they're prompt with the bucket.

In the bathroom, Maeve wipes her mother's face with a damp paper towel, then fills her hands with water and lifts them to her mother's lips. "Do you want to rinse your mouth, Ma?"

Her mother nods, sips the water but, instead of spitting it out, swallows it. "It was an accident," Effie says.

"Of course it was, Ma. No one thinks you threw up on purpose."

Effie shakes her head. She looks like she might say more, but she just closes her eyes.

"It's okay, Ma," Maeve says again.

Maeve has to pee but she doesn't dare leave her mother unattended. Her bladder pushes mercilessly against the zipper of her pants.

When they get back to the table, Peter has paid and Paige is gone. "I let her take the car," Peter says. "Figured I could hitch a ride with you two."

"Did she take the cake, too?"

Even after the vomit episode, Maeve wants a piece of ice cream cake. Which probably speaks to her depravity.

Peter salutes her. "Roger. Cake and teen in car."

Maeve would not have let her drive alone and at night this soon after getting her license, but she obviously has no say. She feels tears again and bats them back with her lids.

Effie says, "She seems like a nice girl." Maeve can smell her mother's vomit and she checks her shoes, her pants, her mother's hands. But she can't see anything.

33

Either she's never noticed the vein on Peter's forehead, or it's new. Maeve closes her eyes, tries to enjoy the sensation of him inside her. Can veins appear out of nowhere? Is it a skull fracture? Does he have a tumor that's rearranging his facial features?

Peter says, "Are you here?"

Maeve laughs, "Who else do you think it is?" She imagines herself taller, blonder, that she's wearing Collette's bracelets, that she's Collette. She refocuses, kisses his neck, runs her hands up and down his back. Maeve pulls him down by the head and then worries she's made the tumor worse.

How fast do tumors grow? And suddenly, she sees Peter in his casket, dozens of lily-based flower arrangements around him, a spray of white roses in his hands with a blue banner: Dad.

"Are you crying?" Peter whispers.

"I'm just happy," she lies. "I've missed you."

This satisfies him enough that he moves ahead to completion.

He told her he was proud of her for getting Paige a therapist so quickly and someone with whom Paige "connected."

Peter kisses Maeve's shoulders, one and then the other. "Now your turn," he says.

She's read the self-help articles in Cosmopolitan while in line at the grocery checkout. She knows she's supposed to be able to tell her man what she likes and what she doesn't. She's absolutely not supposed to fake an orgasm or just get it over with. She manages a little moan of pleasure. She tries to think of the pottery scene in Ghost, because usually that works for her, but she can't see Patrick Swayze's hands, only the wonky lump of clay and that just makes her sad.

Maeve's body feels like it belongs to someone else. A nun, perhaps. "I'm good," she says. "I'm okay." She takes his hand away from where's it's headed and laces her fingers through it as if holding hands with a person who is on top of you is both comfortable and natural.

"Are you sure?" He asks.

Some husbands, she's heard on talk shows, only care about their own pleasure. Maeve should be grateful for Peter's solicitousness. But, right now, it makes her want to smother him with a pillow.

"I'm exhausted," Maeve says. She's careful not to complain too much. She likes to pretend she has it all under control. All okey-dokey.

He rubs a thumb along the purple circles under her eyes. "I see that," he says. He kisses her forehead.

*****

It's one o'clock in the morning and she's wide awake. Maeve pulls the comforter up to her chin and thinks how "comforter" is a bit of an exaggeration. She turns, then turns again, knowing Peter will wake. He does, pulling her into his chest. Maeve says, "When Clipper died, my father was supposed to be watching him. He and Charlie and Anita were putting on some kind of presentation—they were filming it so they could watch it back and see how they could do it better—and my mother went to the grocery store for something for dinner. Clipper ran out into the road and got hit by a car."

"That's terrible." He doesn't ask why she's telling him this now.

"My mother cried for a week. Her eyes were swollen shut." Maeve takes a breath. He still doesn't ask why she's telling him this at one o'clock in the morning. It's possible he's fallen back to sleep. "I think we should get a dog. It'll be good for my mother and it might be good for Paige, too."

"Is that what's keeping you awake?" He squeezes her hand. After a pause, he says, "I'm not sure we have time for a dog."

He doesn't mention the panic attack Maeve had at Cinemagic, but she can feel him thinking that she doesn't need the stress of one more thing. She knows he thinks she's fragile, and Maeve hates being thought of that way. "A dog might be good for me," she says, which she knows is unfair, but might also be true.

When he falls back to sleep, Maeve carries her laptop to the living room. A dog will make them all feel better. Even her father loved Clipper. And Paige loves dogs. She's never asked for one, which is weird because all kids ask for a dog, but maybe she just never thought to ask for one. Maeve browses websites with adoptable dogs and finds a bunch that are small and white with poufy ears and could pass for Clipper. She flags a few to look at again tomorrow.

Somewhere before sunrise, there's a black hole of time in which she finds herself browsing rape forums and blogs.

She reads about a woman forced to have anal sex with her boyfriend.

She reads about a girl fingered by her boss in his office.

She reads about a woman attacked in her dorm room by her study partner, and another by a stranger.

At a party. At work. In a park. In the gym.

She reads about women who said "no" and women who said nothing.

Finally, she closes out of the rape forums, gets off the floor, and, in the kitchen, makes herself tea and resumes her search for Clipper. At seven, she texts Dr. B and tells him she has a family emergency, which is an excuse he must be getting tired of. At 7:04, he texts back to tell her to take all the time she needs.

By eight she's showered, kissed Peter, and told him Flora will be there by nine. Maeve says she's going to a dental conference. She insists she told Peter all about it last week. She says he never listens to her. She's a terrible liar—a guilty, flush-faced, liar—and so she says all this while she brushes her teeth. Still, her face has pinked and Peter must know, but he doesn't press her. He probably thinks she needs some time to herself.

By ten she's at the Portsmouth Humane Society, filling out paperwork and forking over two hundred bucks for a little white dog. They're at capacity, the woman says, rubbing the straw-like hair beneath her baseball cap. Usually there's a waiting period and a reference check. Maeve smiles her front-desk smile and writes down Collette as a reference.

It will be good mother-daughter bonding time for her and Paige to walk the dog. She imagines looping the neighborhood, Clipper trotting along between them.

The dog is quiet on the way back, so much so that Maeve stops at the rest stop in Kennebunk to make sure he hasn't died. He hasn't. She fastens his leash and lifts him out of the car and he dutifully sniffs around and lifts his leg. He ignores the other dogs and Maeve wonders if there's something wrong with him, but what does it matter now?

She says, "Good boy, Clipper." And when he looks at her, she bursts into tears.

34

Maeve has been in her bedroom with the shades drawn, sitting cross-legged on the floor and breathing deeply. Wendy suggested meditation, and Maeve agreed to three minutes a day, thinking one hundred and eighty seconds of quiet is not unreasonable. And yet, her brain is like a pinball game—her mother, her father, Paige, Anita.

Yesterday, she had the dog in her arms in the kitchen when Peter got home.

"I thought you were at a dental conference," he said. He kissed her cheek and rubbed Clipper's head, but there was a field of anger around him, something she almost never felt from Peter, and something that made her immediately defensive.

"I really needed to do this and you would have said no."

Peter looked at her sadly and said, "I'm only trying to help here, Maeve."

When Maeve releases herself from the three minutes, she finds Effie in the living room. She has untied the curtains and is pulling them closed.

"Are you cold, Mom?"

Effie jumps and turns. Her face is all fury and Maeve tries to remember what she's read about how to re-orient someone. Ask her what's wrong? Don't ask her? "You're home, Mom," she says. Which isn't true. They're in Maeve's home, in Maeve's living room, and if Effie were still Effie, she'd know this isn't her home. Yesterday, her mother petted Clipper and when

Maeve told her his name she said, "Isn't that funny." Today, she's asked Maeve twice who the dog belongs to.

Is she supposed to move closer to her mother or stay where she is? "Effie," she says. Maybe calling her "Mom" is confusing because maybe Effie doesn't know Maeve as her daughter right now. Yesterday, she called her Grace twice, which caused Maeve to touch her hair to see if she'd become a different person. She remembered not to say that Grace died years ago of ovarian cancer.

Effie shakes her head. "I don't want that woman here."

"What woman?" Maeve strains to see around her mother. "Was someone selling raffle tickets again?"

Effie narrows her eyes. "You know who I mean."

Maeve has no idea who her mother means. She wedges a smile into her voice. "Was it too bright with the curtains open?"

"It was something." Effie storms to the dining room, yanking the sheer curtains across. "Do you have sheets? Blankets?"

Maeve thinks about the time they were expecting a hurricane—Bob, maybe?—and her father nailed plywood on the windows. It had been like the inside of a coffin. "Is it the snow that's bothering you?"

Effie stares out the window and Maeve follows her gaze. It isn't snowing, hasn't snowed all week, but what's on the ground is crusty and bright with ice. Directly into Maeve's ear, like when she was a child and Effie would say she loved her to the moon, Effie says, "She looks in. She must. She said something just last week about how she noticed the results of the Jane Fonda video I was doing." Effie is holding the curtain in her fist.

Maeve feels a fissure of anxiety from neck to toes. She

means Anita. Maeve remembers her mother telling her she ran into Anita at the grocery store—it must have been when Maeve was seventeen or eighteen, just about to leave for college. It had been at least a year since Maeve had seen Anita and the mention of her name made her ache with sadness she knew better than to let her mother see. That day, Maeve said something about her mother always being defensive, always thinking Anita was being mean when she wasn't. Now, she says, "Maybe she was trying to compliment you."

Effie scoffs. "They think they can make me feel bad about myself." Effie makes a gesture indicating big hair.

Maeve strokes the back of her mother's head which feels matted with shampoo not quite rinsed out. Someone walking by must have looked like Anita, or maybe Effie had a dream. "They work together. That's all." She isn't going to bring Anita up by name.

Effie shakes her head. "Grace told me and told me—don't be a fool, she said." She's angry now, tears streaking her papery cheeks. "And you, acting like she's the best thing since skim milk."

There's a knock and they both turn. Maeve half expects it to be Anita Haverland, back from the dead, and she's so relieved when it's Paige that she doesn't register her mother saying "This one is probably some friend of hers." Maeve steps forward but Effie grabs her shoulder and pulls her back, pulls her right up against her so that Maeve thinks she'll topple both of them. How is her mother—her tiny, unsteady mother—this strong? Through the gauzy curtain that frames the window of the front door, Paige watches them.

Maeve says, "It's Paige. I think she's forgotten her key."

Clipper barks and whines.

"She could have sent a friend to get pictures of me like this," Effie says. Her breath smells like pickled beets and is damp against Maeve's cheek. Effie wears a pale blue sweatshirt Maeve bought her at Goodwill last week. She hasn't had her hair done in months. The last time Maeve took her to the hairdressers, Effie refused to pay because she said the hairdresser made her look like an old woman.

"It's your granddaughter," Maeve says. She pulls away as gently as she can, but she can see the marks her nails have left on her mother's papery hands. A constellation of crescent moons that will bloom into bruises.

"I do not have grandchildren. You're as bad as she is, trying to make me believe things." Effie's teeth are clenched, her hands fisted. "Why don't you just mind your own business?"

When Maeve opens the door, Paige is all breath and cold air and sliding out of her boots and jacket. Maeve doesn't see Effie lurch forward—in part because she would have never expected her mother could still move so fast—and before she has time to even put out a hand to stop her, Effie launches herself at Paige. She yanks her hair, then pulls her all the way down to the ground. Paige's face contorts with pain and shock. Clipper inserts himself in the melee, licking, wagging, barking. He thinks they're playing, but Maeve knows they're not. Paige mewls like a baby and Maeve wraps her arms around her mother's middle, tags. "Mom," she says. "Mom, Mom." When the pulling doesn't have any effect, she reaches over and untangles her mother's hands from Paige's hair, and finally, finally Paige rolls away and stands. Effie hisses and spits like a wild animal.

"You're all right," she says when Paige looks at her, tear-streaked and angry. "You'll be all right."

Paige doesn't ask Maeve how she could let this happen. She flees upstairs without another word, Clipper following close behind her. Paige will for sure tell her therapist this.

"Where did that dog come from?" Effie asks, smoothing down the wrinkled front of her daisy-patterned housedress.

35

Stewart says, "This isn't your fault."

Maeve's walking into work and she would hang up on Stewart except that her phone is tucked between her ear and shoulder and she's carrying her lunch in one hand, her work bag in the other.

He says, "Have you checked to see where she is on the waiting list?"

He says, "Dad says she's really confused."

He says, "Paige must have been terrified."

He says, "Maybe the dog wasn't such a good idea."

Maeve says, "Have you ever wanted a time machine?"

"What?"

"Nevermind."

He says, "Mild Brook isn't such a bad place."

He says, "I didn't know Ma had it in her."

"Maeve?"

"I'm walking into work."

And then she stashes her purse under her desk and hangs her coat in the break room and she's all Good Morning and Have a Nice Day.

*****

That night, her father comes for dinner. Peter has made Shepherd's Pie and Paige eats three bites and then says she isn't hungry. They aren't the kind of parents who have ever required their kid to ask permission before getting up from the table, and so Paige pushes away, kisses her grandmother and grandfather, and says she has homework.

They listen to her door close. Peter clears his throat. "I don't know if Maeve already told you—"

Maeve shoots him a look.

Peter meets her gaze but goes on anyway, even though she can tell he's registered her meaning. What good will it do to tell Tom what happened between Paige and Effie? Also, she hates talking about Effie in front of Effie. Peter says, "Paige was attacked by her, uh, grandmother."

This is his way of not saying Effie's name because they all know Effie doesn't remember she's Paige's grandmother. She usually thinks Paige is a sweet girl. Sometimes she mistakes her for Maeve or Grace.

Tom looks up, fork full of corn and mashed potatoes.

Peter says, "It was pretty bad. There was hitting, grabbing. It was intense."

Effie has submerged her napkin in her water glass and is now drinking it, as if this is the most natural thing in the world. The water spills out all around the napkin, very little of it making it into her mouth.

Tom sets down his fork and stares into his plate. "That must have been very scary for Paige."

This isn't what Maeve expected him to say and she's so stunned she can feel her jaw unhinge. He's not surprised.

Peter says, "Yes, it really was. We wanted you to know, obviously."

"Right," Tom says. He pushes back his chair. "Time for bed." This he addresses to Effie, who looks at him with abject horror.

"I can help her wash up," Maeve says.

"It's okay," Tom says. He holds out his hand and Effie takes it and, after a long minute, follows him. Maeve isn't sure what to make of her father's insistence or her mother's compliance. She and Peter clear the table and, while he's loading the dishwasher, she wanders down the hall. Paige must be texting or reading—she's not crying, anyway. Tom and Effie are talking, quiet and urgent, and Maeve has to stay very still to hear them.

"It's okay," her father says.

"She's after me."

"She's not, Eff." His tone is one of placation. He isn't angry, he isn't frustrated.

"You weren't here."

"She's not going to bother you anymore."

"You don't know that." Effie sniffles. She sounds like a little girl.

"I do know," Tom says. "I can promise you she won't bother you anymore."

"How do you know?" Effie's voice rises and Maeve considers going in, interrupting to ask if they want dessert or if her father needs toothpaste. She doesn't want to know what's going on. She could just walk away. There's a long silence and Maeve swears she can hear the rustle of hands on fabric, as if he's rubbing Effie's back, like Maeve would sometimes see him do when she came into the kitchen. Arms wrapped around each other in a hug, his hands making circles on her back.

Finally, Effie asks, "Is she dead?"

This startles Maeve, but if it surprises Tom, he doesn't show it in his voice. He is very tender when he says, "Yes."

"Did I do it?"

"It was an accident, Eff."

She sniffles and gulps. "I'm sorry."

"I know you are."

"I didn't mean it."

"I know."

Maeve feels as though she's turned to ash. Like she might be a heap on the floor Peter finds in the morning and vacuums up. Everything she's known to be true—everything that has come together to create her—has just shifted. Her mother pushed Anita and her father has known and protected her. From the police. From Maeve. From herself.

Peter calls, "Honey, where's the dish detergent?

Maeve stumbles away from the door, back down the hall, and into the kitchen. "Sorry," she says. "I moved it." She pulls a chair over to the refrigerator, climbs up, and retrieves the Cascade from the very back. So that her mother doesn't mistake it for sugar and top her oatmeal with it.

Peter says, "You do that every time you run the dishwasher?"

"It's just for now," Maeve says.

36

Maeve is sixteen and trying to convince her mother to let her take her picture. "You don't have to do anything except what you'd normally do," Maeve says. Since she opened it on her birthday, Maeve has hardly let the Cannon Sure Shot out of her hands.

Effie shakes her head. "Why would you want a picture of me doing dishes?"

"It's going to be a series of candids," Maeve says.

When she told Anita her idea, Anita tilted her head and said, "Taking pictures of people can be very intimate. Especially if they don't know you're there."

The word "intimate" made Maeve blush, but she nodded and said, "Sure. That's art, isn't it?"

Now, Effie says, "Find someone else." She smiles when she says this, though, and rolls her eyes. As if she might be joking, might entertain the possibility of letting Maeve take her picture. With a sponge and hands not gloved by the kind of long rubber pink ones Anita Haverland wears, she scrubs at the pot she used to make chili, which they ate with cornbread last night.

Maeve drags a chair over to the sink and climbs on top of it. Effie slides her eyes towards her, but says nothing. Maeve wants to see both what is and isn't there, although she can't really explain what she means by this. She bends at the waist, then the knees. She snaps shot after shot.

When Effie rinses the pot and upends it on the draining board, Maeve goes in for a shot of her face. Effie turns away. "That's enough. I mean it, Maeve. Why don't you see what Collette's up to this afternoon?"

Stewart took his girlfriend to see Cape Fear, which is still playing at the Parker Cinemagic. Her father is at a New Year New You conference, even though the new year is still three weeks away. So, Maeve huffs it next door and asks Collette if she can take a few candids of her. It snowed five inches this morning, and Collette looks up from the path she's clearing from the backdoor to the shed and smiles. Collette moved in next door the year before last and Effie calls her a "bachelorette," which makes Maeve think of parties. Effie says she doesn't understand why Collette is "tying herself down" with a mortgage when she might marry someone who doesn't want to live in their "family-oriented" neighborhood. She's also constantly encouraging Maeve to see if Collette wants to go for a walk or to a movie. "She's someone you could look up to," Effie has said more than once. Maeve isn't stupid—she knows Effie means "instead of Anita" and it isn't like she doesn't like Collette. She just doesn't like her the same way she likes Anita. Collette doesn't have the same sparkle, even though Maeve would never say that out loud because it makes her sound like a ten-year-old.

"Just keep doing what you're doing," Maeve says. "I'm working on an art project. It's a series of candids." Her mother would tell her to put down her camera and help Collette shovel, for god's sake. But Effie can't see Maeve and so Maeve snaps one picture after another.

But, even when Maeve shoots her from behind so that she's all plaid jacket with a burst of blonde hair on top, Collette keeps glancing over her shoulder, smiling, and, once, even waving.

Maybe it's Collette's very niceness that Maeve finds off-putting. Anita has more edges.

"Pretend I'm not here," Maeve says, and then says again. She thinks of Anita's photographs of inanimate objects and how much easier that seems. Still, without her camera, Maeve would never have come over here, even though Collette has never been anything but happy to see her. Without the camera, she would not have seen sweet, poised Collette stick out her tongue and roll her eyes and give Maeve the hang loose sign over her shoulder. Maeve is thrilled by Collette's agreeableness.

"Do you know the woman my father works with? Anita Haverland?" Maeve asks. Collette pauses to give her a wide-eyed grin. She's not sure what she wants Collette to say, only that she wants to talk about how much she's been learning from Anita, and how much she likes her.

"I know *of* her," Collette says.

"From my Mom?"

Collette nods.

"Ma hates her." Maeve can say this because she's safely behind the camera, safely not looking at Collette.

Collette tips her head to her shoulder. "She has her reasons, but hate is a strong word, honey." In that moment, Collette reminds Maeve of her Aunt Grace, who died two years ago from cancer, and suddenly Maeve wonders if people are just versions of other people superimposed on one another.

Maeve takes picture after picture even though she's no longer seeing Collette, but Aunt Grace, then Effie, and then Anita. After a while, Maeve says, "It makes me feel bad for being her friend, but I don't want to not be her friend. She's never done anything to me."

Collette goes back to shoveling and Maeve senses she doesn't like what she just said.

Finally, Collette says, "It's okay to like people your parents don't like. It'll probably happen more and more as you grow up."

Maeve nods as if she understands this. Collette, at thirty-something, seems old—although not as old as her parents—and wise to Maeve.

After ten more minutes of Collette shoveling and turning, winking and smiling, Maeve thanks her and trudges home.

She's just rounded the corner when her father's car pulls into the driveway. When Maeve was little, she would run to him from wherever she was—the bedroom, the kitchen, the yard—and throw herself at him. He would lift her up and twirl her until she got too big to be lifted, and then he would kneel on the ground and catch and blow raspberries on her neck.

She was ten or eleven when she stopped. One day, she ran to him and, instead of swooping her up, he put his arm around her in a half-hug and said, "You're getting' kind of big for all the fuss, huh?"

Maybe he hadn't meant for her to stop going to him entirely, but she did.

Now, she watches him get out of the car, open the trunk, remove his briefcase and a box. He's moving as though he's underwater and Maeve lifts her camera and snaps a picture. He looks sad, but that doesn't stop her.

He doesn't go in through the front door, which is the way he always goes in. He always leaves his shoes in the corner between the mat and the wall and swaggers into the kitchen and kisses Effie and pats Clipper and pulls down a mug and the bottle of Captain's.

This time, he goes in through the garage. Maeve takes the front door. Her mother is folding laundry in the living room. Maeve lifts her camera and says, "Dad's home."

She snaps the picture as her mother looks up at the clock. "It's three," Effie says. "I'm going to take that camera away from you if you don't knock it off."

Maeve tucks the camera behind her back and wanders into the kitchen for a Haverland Health cracker with a smear of peanut butter. Maeve chews the cracker, which really is more rice cake than cracker, and waits. Soon enough her mother calls up the stairs asking her father if he's home and he calls down that he is.

"Are you sick?" She asks. She heads up the stairs, laundry basket on her hip. Maeve takes one, two, three shots from behind and her mother doesn't turn around even though Maeve's sure she's heard the clatter of the shutter.

Maeve rolls the film strip and loads another cannister of film. She pads up the stairs and stands in the hallway, just out of sight, like she's some kind of photographer Nancy Drew.

In the bedroom, her mother stands by the dresser so that she's reflected back into the room. She says, "What's wrong?"

Maeve can't see her father, but she hears him say, "Charlie made some cuts."

Her mother frowns. "Cuts? Why? I thought they were doing a good business."

"Times are tough, Ef."

Her mother moves away from the dresser and Maeve hears the rustle of the comforter when her mother sits on the bed. "You love that job."

"I'll figure out something."

"I don't understand how they can do this to you. You've

worked for the Haverlands for years."

"It's just business," Tom says. To Maeve, he sounds very far away, as if he's buried his face in the pillows.

"Is it temporary, do you think?"

"Leave it alone, Effie."

They're quiet for a while before her father says, "I'll figure out something."

"Stewart starts college in the fall."

And then her father is in front of the dresser, crossing the room, slamming the door with such force the house rattles. "Give me some credit!" He roars. "Give me a fucking minute before you start in on me!"

Maeve flees. Down the hallway, through the kitchen, out the door, into the snow. She's still cradling the camera against her chest when she reaches her mother's car. Her mother keeps her keys in the car so she doesn't lose them, which Maeve has always found irresponsible but now she finds helpful.

At first, she's thinking of just getting away. And then, when she's started the car and backed down the driveway and neither of her parents have come to the door, she thinks about going to the Haverlands' and asking Anita what happened. She'll just ring the bell and ask, friend to friend. Because they're friends. They are.

Charlie's truck is in the driveway, which means that after he sent Maeve's father home, Charlie went home, which might be a good sign—a sign that he's upset about whatever happened and if he's upset, maybe it can be undone. He's the boss, after all. Maeve parks at the top of the driveway and walks down, because their driveway is long and narrow and hard to turn around in when someone is already parked in it. She can hear them on the deck and she imagines their words frozen in little puffs between them. There's no pause in their conversation, no hesitation. They haven't heard her.

Years later, she'll wonder about this moment. She'll wonder who she thought she was, what she thought she could accomplish, why she didn't think she might be invading the Haverlands' privacy, and why she thought it so important to know what happened. Because whatever happened had already happened and there was no undoing it, certainly not by some brazen sixteen-year-old kid. But, in that moment, with the cushioning of snow beneath her boots, Maeve feels both important and invisible.

She walks into the Haverlands' through their unlocked back door. She takes off her boots, pads through the kitchen and down the long hallway. It's dusk now, and she stops before she's out of the shadows. Anita and Charlie face each other on the deck. Her hair is loose around her face, but kinked as though it's recently come down from a bun. His hands are fisted at his chest. This, Maeve thinks, is exactly the kind of moment a real photographer looks for—the raw emotion, the unguarded expressions. Never has she seen Anita Haverland look more vulnerable or beautiful. Maeve raises her camera and takes a picture.

Charlie says, "You embarrassed me." The glass slider is open, as if they've been too distracted to close it behind them.

Anita says, "I doubt it. I doubt you even care." Her face is marble, but her voice is all cracked glass.

The moment the shutter clicks is also the moment the Haverlands' both pause to catch their breath. At the sound, Anita cocks her head. Charlie starts to say something, but Anita holds up a hand and Maeve sees that one of her perfect pink nails is broken. Anita turns and steps into the hallway where

Maeve has stopped breathing, as if that will make her disappear.

Anita looks at her, looks at the camera. "Ah," she says. She holds out her hand, the one without the broken nail, and Maeve hands her the camera.

"What happened?" Maeve asks. Although she knows, all of a sudden and with perfect clarity. Charlie found out about Anita and Tom—about whatever has been going on between them which Maeve knows vaguely is an affair but which she can't acknowledge, not yet—and, because of that, he's fired Tom. What Maeve means is, "How could this happen?" And "How did you not know this would happen?" And "What happens now?"

Anita opens the camera's back, pulls out the film, keeps pulling until it's one long exposed strip. She hands the camera and the useless length of film back to Maeve.

"You've been lying to me," Maeve says.

Anita shakes her head.

Maeve's throat clogs with tears and even though she swallows and swallows, her nose pinches and there's no stopping the tears. She expects Anita to at least say she's sorry, a sorry that might encompass many things, but Anita just turns and walks back out to the deck.

Maeve screeches at her, as if she's a very small child. "You're not my friend. You've never been my friend."

Anita turns and looks at Maeve for a long moment. Maybe there's a flash of regret, but Maeve can't register it. What she sees is the blank blink of someone who hasn't ever really cared. "Maybe someday you'll understand," Anita says.

"No," Maeve says. "I won't." And then, out of some kind of desperate humiliation, she adds with as much viciousness as she can muster, "I hate you."

37

"What is it you want?" Wendy asks her.

"For none of this to have happened." The room is as hot as a whistling teakettle and Maeve is sweating in her Parker, ME sweatshirt, a sweatshirt Peter bought her as if she might forget where she lives. Her mother should have it. Maybe Maeve will give it to her. She considers taking it off, but she isn't wearing a bra and her t-shirt is thin and damp with sweat.

"Peter says we have to *do* something—that it's not safe for Effie to keep living with us." And she hasn't even told him what she heard Tom and Effie talking about last night. Will her husband—who lives by the strictest of moral codes—insist they call the police and tell them what Effie has done? He might not listen to Maeve if Maeve says the right thing and the legal thing aren't always one and the same. She hasn't told Wendy, either, because she wants her on her side. This is, Maeve knows, not the right way to do therapy. Or marriage.

"And you think differently?" Wendy asks. Pinned to Wendy's gray blazer is a gold bunny brooch. It's discreet, but the nod to Easter annoys Maeve. How does Wendy have enough time to match her brooches to the seasons?

Maeve says, "He's been so protective of Paige."

"Since the rape?"

Maeve winces. "Sure. Yes."

This morning, Maeve exchanged the purse for the one Paige actually wanted—which Paige showed her online—and returned the fluffy white sweater Peter bought her. She considered buying something she really wants, like a wool coat or a few good bras, but the mall was crowded and she couldn't handle another minute of heat and body odor and the general hum of humanity. She accepted a gift card in exchange for her sweater, knowing full well she'll forget she has it until someday, years from now, the store will go out of business before Maeve cleans out her purse and finds the unredeemed card.

Wendy folds her hands and drops her head. Maybe they'll pray. Maybe Maeve will pray for a full night's sleep. Wendy says, "What about what you want, realistically?"

"A time machine."

Wendy laughs like Maeve has the capacity to delight her. "Not exactly realistic, but okay. Where would it take you?"

A better version of Maeve would say she wants to go back to before Kris raped Paige or to before her mother attacked Paige or to before her mother pushed Anita down the basement stairs. "To when I was a kid," Maeve says.

Maeve should take the sweatshirt off. Her t-shirt underneath is navy blue so it isn't like Wendy will see anything and even if she does, will she care? She's a doctor of sorts, so she must have had to take anatomy. But, last week, Maeve had been freezing during her appointment and so she's certain Wendy has turned up the heat just for her and it will seem ungrateful to be too hot now.

"Is there a specific moment you'd go back to?"

Maeve should have thought through her answer better. She doesn't really want to talk about her childhood right now. Could she get up and leave in the middle of a therapy session? That might be the kind of thing that raises "concerns" about your mental well-being, and Maeve would rather not. "When

I was eight, my mother asked me to walk with her to the grocery store. It was only a couple of miles away, but there weren't any sidewalks, so I wasn't allowed to go by myself. Usually, I jumped at the chance to go with her, but I was in the middle of building this really elaborate Barbie house out of folded towels and Dixie cups so I said no." Maeve wishes she brought a water bottle. She says, "She put on her boots and went without me."

"Do you think she was hurt by your refusal?"

Maeve nods, although she isn't sure. She would have, up until this moment, said her mother had been angry, but "hurt" makes it seem as though Maeve had some agency in the incident, which is probably Wendy's point. The nodding causes a waterfall of sweat down her back. "Before she left, she told me not to open the door for anyone, not to use the stove, not to go outside." Maeve licks her dry lips with her dry tongue. "It's funny because that's what we tell her now." Maeve can feel this hysterical, pre-panic laughter, and she swallows it down. "Anyway. Stewart and my Dad were at a hockey game in Portland. For the first five minutes, I was thrilled to be alone."

Wendy waits a bit. "You felt all grown up."

Even Maeve's feet are sweating now, her socks turning soggy in her boots. "It's not even like I heard a noise or got hungry. I just decided I was done playing and I went after her."

Maeve squints at the clock but she can't see it. Wendy's office is dim and the cuckoo clock on her desk is brown with black numbers. Maeve only knows the time when the little bird pops out on the hour.

Maeve says, "She was walking back and I caught up to her. I don't know what I was thinking. That she'd be delighted, I guess."

"What was her reaction?"

Maeve's face feels like it might catch on fire. She imagines Peter swooping in with the appropriate fire extinguisher. "She was mad."

Wendy waits. The cuckoo ticks.

"She grabbed me by my hood and yanked me along next to her."

"She yanked you?"

"And not just, like, a single tug. She dragged me for—" Maeve is about to say "miles" and then "at least a mile," but as the words form, she knows it was probably only thirty seconds, at the most. "A while," she settles on.

"She was worried about you," Wendy says. "Her reaction wasn't the best, but it sounds like it stemmed for the fear that you'd walked all that way by yourself."

"She said I could have been hit by a car or kidnapped." It was stupid to tell this story because all it does is paint her mother as a person with the potential for violence, and Maeve as someone who never listens.

Wendy asks, "What was your reaction to that?"

"I waited until we got home and then as soon as we walked in the door—she was walking fast and she was ahead of me so I had to catch the door—I stormed in behind her and I just started screaming that she was the worst mother in the world."

Wendy waits. Maeve writes the check for her copay. "I'd go back and not say that," Maeve says.

*****

At first, she tells herself she's just going to drive by Anita's house to check on it. Although there's a part of her that knows her father has been doing that very thing. Keeping the pipes from freezing. Making sure no one breaks in, which would be rare but you never know. He said something the other day about seeing a bald eagle grabbing the remnants of someone's ice fishing. He didn't say where he was when he saw the eagle, but Maeve knew. Maeve turns down the long driveway. How will she explain herself if her father is here now? Maybe she'll tell him she was worried about him, wanted to check on him, went to the Ever-yellow first and he wasn't there. He'll know she's lying.

She knows where the Haverlands keep the key, or where they used to keep the key. If it isn't there anymore, she'll just go home. If it isn't there, it wasn't meant to be. It's there. Tucked into the gap between the left porch light and the wall of the house. She's never gone into Anita's house without her. She only knows where the key is because Anita told her once that she was always welcome there, even if they weren't home. That conversation was in the context of a fight Maeve had with Effie, and, even all these years later, Maeve can feel the bitterness of betrayal in the back of her throat. Maeve opens the door.

Even though the house sits at the end of a long drive-way and is hidden from the neighbors on both sides by dense pine trees, the Haverlands don't have an alarm. Or, they didn't. Maeve holds her breath for a second and when nothing sounds, she exhales. Almost no one in Maine has house alarms, unless you count barking dogs as house alarms.

Inside smells faintly of winter damp and oranges. Maeve's breath squeezes in the way that foretells a panic attack. She does her square breathing until she won't start to cry or laugh or have her breath squeeze tight as a rubber ball.

Maeve takes off her boots and, in her socked feet, wanders from room to room. She looks at the pictures—the sand and peas and pearls right where they've always been. Among her old favorites are new pictures Maeve has to study for a long time to figure out—rose, cherry, peach, coffee. She should be in a hurry. She should worry that her father will show up, or that her mother needs her. But, for the first time in months, Maeve feels like she's exactly where she's supposed to be.

In the freezer, there are Haverland Health Ice Cream bars, which are sugar-free and non-dairy, but Maeve is hungry enough to peel off the stuck-on paper and eat two.

Peter texts her five times asking what she wants for dinner and when she'll be home and if everything is okay and then, finally, a frantic series of question marks. She's trying to come up with a text to let him know she's alright even though she's not completely alright, when he calls. At first, she thinks about not answering, but that seems cruel and she isn't a cruel person.

He says, "Are you okay?" Before she can even say hello.

She says, "I'm fine."

He pauses. "You sound funny."

Maeve takes a hitchy breath. "It's not fair that Stewart gets to live in California. That he doesn't have to deal with any of this unless he gets on a plane and how often does he do that?"

"Where are you, honey?"

In the pantry, Maeve finds a jar of shelled pistachios and tosses a handful into her mouth. They're rankly spoiled and she spits them into her palm. It soothes her that the nuts are spoiled. It means her father hasn't been making everything okay over here.

"Are you eating?" Peter asks.

"Just a snack," she says.

"Where are you?"

Maeve fishes the stuck nut-remnants out of her gums. Finally, Peter says, "I get it if you need a night to recharge your batteries, but you can't not tell me. I was really worried about you."

This makes her want to laugh and cry. That he thinks she's left him with her mother and that he's not even angry. "I'm sorry," she says.

"You'll come home tomorrow?"

"I will." She's not sure she will. If she stays here in Anita's big house, it's possible no one will find her. She'll go to the grocery store in disguise. She'll keep the lights off at night. She'll have to hide her car somewhere. If she doesn't go home, Stewart will have to come back from California. He'll have to stay with Effie.

She falls asleep in the guest bedroom thinking about what it would be like to live as a kind of ghost in this house forever.

It's her father who finds her in the morning. She's still wrapped in Anita's cream-colored robe, her green avocado face mask on her face, a white towel turbanning her hair. He lets himself in. Because he has his own key, of course.

"Peter's worried sick about you," he says.

He isn't surprised to find her there, and this makes Maeve furious. Is she so predictable? Has she always been this wrapped up in Anita that her father knew exactly where to look? Maeve says, "I told him I was alright. How did you know I was here?"

"But you didn't sound alright." He goes to the fridge and takes out a beer, pops the top, drinks. "Your car was in the driveway. I was coming to water the plants. I told the real estate agent I'd try not to let anything die." He stops as if realizing what he's just said. It's ten o'clock in the morning. Is beer what he drinks when he's not drinking rum? Maeve doesn't know and she doesn't really want to know, because knowing would mean she has to do something, even if that something

229

is pretending she doesn't know.

"You spend a lot of time here?" Maeve asks.

He shrugs as he finishes the beer, rinses the can, tosses it into the recycling bin under the sink. "I did. Before your Mom started needing me at home more."

Maeve snorts. "Is that supposed to make you some kind of hero? That you stopped spending so much time with your mistress after your wife started having strokes?" He shakes his head. "You're going to make me out to be the bad guy no matter what I say."

"Because you *are* the bad guy."

Tom lifts his baseball cap and rubs his thinning hair. "Maybe I am."

"I don't get why you didn't just leave Mom and marry Anita." The face mask is starting to itch. Maeve crosses to the kitchen sink, turns on the tap, and splashes her face. Greenish water flies everywhere, which she'll have to clean up. Although what does it matter? Anita and Charlie won't ever live here again.

Tom says, "Your mother—she was always…fragile. I didn't ever think I could leave her."

Maeve rips off a paper towel and sandpapers her face dry. "You could have stopped seeing Anita."

Tom gives a single nod. "I could have."

He doesn't say it, but Maeve can feel it hanging between them. *But I loved her.*

Maeve turns back to the sink to scrub the green off her hands. "None of this would have happened if you'd stopped seeing Anita. She wouldn't have been at the house. Mom wouldn't have hated her. Anita would still be alive right now if you had just ended this stupid affair years and years ago. I gave her up—why couldn't you give her up?" Maeve has her back to her father and she's crying, the tears running into what's left of the mask and sending streaks of green down her chest and all over Anita's pristine bathrobe. When Maeve takes a breath, she thinks she can hear her father crying, too.

"It was selfish," he says finally. "But Anita didn't want to end it, either. I know you don't believe me, but we loved each other. And I love your mother. It's complicated, Maeve. I'm sorry."

His apology is the thing Maeve never thought she'd get and it loosens something in her. Her crying turns ugly and she sags against the counter, letting herself sob.

Tom gets another beer out of the fridge. He pulls out the silver leather barstool and sits in a way he's probably sat a thousand times. He doesn't tell Maeve to get herself together. He just sits there and drinks his beer and waits. When she's exhausted her tears, Maeve looks up to see if he's watching her, but he isn't. He's looking out the big sliding glass doors, to the lake, where an eagle is swopping over an abandoned ice fishing hole. It dives down, then rears up, a fish in it's talons. "Isn't that something," Tom says.

"It really is," Maeve sniffles.

38

When Cindy the Social Worker calls to say there's an opening at Mild Brook, Maeve can't think of any reasonable way to turn it down. She calls Stewart after she hangs up with Cindy, who sounds delighted that Effie will be "joining" them, as if she's starting Girl Scouts.

Stewart says, "It's absolutely the right thing."

Maeve says, "Then you tell her."

"Everything will be fine," he says.

"Everything is always fine in California."

"What do you want, Maeve? Do you want me to uproot my life in California just to come home and help you take care of Ma?" It's the first time she's heard the edge of frustration in his voice and she feels a glimmer of satisfaction at this.

And then, emboldened by her satisfaction, she says, "It's a little late for that, don't you think? Maybe if you had come home, we could have kept her out of the nursing home."

He's quiet for a long time. Then, gently, he says, "Do you really think so?"

Maeve softens. "I don't know. No. Probably not."

He tells her he loves her and that he's here for her and to call whenever she needs to talk and then they hang up and Maeve feels worse than before she called him.

The nursing home powers-that-be don't give you any lead time, probably because too many people change their minds. The very next day, Peter and Maeve tell Effie they're taking her for a ride. Then they tell her they're stopping at Mild Brook because they have a friend they'd like to visit. Peter is the one who says this because, even though they planned and rehearsed to have Maeve say it, when the time comes, the words are stuck like flies to glue.

When they get to Mild Brook, Effie says, "I'll wait here." She closes her eyes and leans her head back.

"It's too cold, Ma," Peter says. "Come in with us for just a few minutes."

Effie sighs but lets him take her arm and lead her in. She loves Peter, and that makes what they're about to do so much worse.

Earlier in the day, Maeve brought Effie's clothes, her cold cream, soap, and a new twin bedspread patterned with tiny yellow tulips. Cindy has given them instructions to take Effie to the music program, sit with her for a bit and then, when she's distracted, leave. They'll handle the rest, Cindy has promised.

"My father should be the one doing this," Maeve murmurs to Peter.

This morning, her father called, and, his words slushing together, said he couldn't do it. "I can't abandon her in that place," he said. "I know I'm a coward."

Peter squeezes her hand, letting her know he heard her, but they need to carry on.

In Mild Brook's huge, high-ceilinged living room, there's a woman in a black evening gown playing a keyboard. She's singing the most upbeat version of *Danny Boy* Maeve has ever heard—not that she's heard all that many versions—to a sea of limp white heads.

"Let's sit and listen to this for a bit," Maeve says to Effie, as if the idea has only this minute occurred to her. As if it's perfectly natural to arrive somewhere you hadn't planned to be and then just settle in for a bit.

Effie looks at Maeve like she's crazy and Maeve thinks maybe she is. "I'd like to go home," Effie says.

There are three seats at the back, probably meant for them, and Peter flops down in the one closest to a woman with her head on her chest, lightly snoring. He pats the seat next to him.

"Just for a few minutes," Maeve says. She tries to signal to Peter to let Effie in first so they can make their quick exit, but he's too busy singing along with the few residents who are awake. Maeve sits and Effie sits beside her. They'll have to climb over her to leave. How on earth will they get away? Maeve imagines them all here tonight, the three of them tucked into Effie's single hospital bed with the quilt Maeve brought from home barely covering them.

They sit through *When Irish Eyes Are Smilin'*, and *In the Good Old Summertime*. The singer's black gown is made of something that looks like crushed velvet. She has her hair down and wears necklaces in silver and gold that reach the proximity of her belly button. When she starts in on *You Are My Sunshine*, which Effie sang to Maeve and Maeve sang to Paige, the tears rush out of Maeve like someone has moved a boulder away from her tear ducts. She touches Effie's arm. "I need a tissue."

Maeve half-stands and scoots past Effie and into the bathroom, which is clean and sterile. When she comes out, Peter's there. "Are you ready to go?" He asks.

Maeve wants to say no, she's not ready. She's changed her mind. Maybe they can figure this out. Maybe she can be a better daughter.

But she says none of that and they leave. Maeve can see the slight bob of her mother's head as she follows along to the music. They walk through the lobby and Maeve thinks that if Effie turns, she'll go get her. But Effie doesn't turn and Maeve and Peter walk out of the lobby and into the cold afternoon.

*****

At home, Maeve waits to feel disoriented, adrift, ashamed. A better daughter would feel all of those things.

Sometimes, she walks into a room expecting to see her mother and is startled when she's not there. Sometimes, she hears her singing the chickadee song only to realize it's just the TV or dishwasher.

Her father has come over twice for dinner and eaten what she's put in front of him without complaint and asked Peter how work was going and asked Paige if she's started thinking about colleges. Maeve hasn't asked him how he's holding up because she wants him to ask her. She doesn't bother telling that to Wendy.

*****

It takes less than a month for Cindy the social worker to say Effie needs a wheelchair because she's too unsteady on her feet and forgets to use the walker. Mild Brook will provide the wheelchair—she just wants Maeve to not be surprised when she next comes in to visit.

Maeve gets to Mild Brook on a Tuesday after work to find her mother standing, one arm braced on her wheelchair, the other extended in front of her, holding a bra. "Help me hang this," she says when she sees Maeve.

Maeve locks the brakes on the wheelchair. Mild Brook has a policy about not using restraints unless a person is in "grave danger."

Effie says, "No one hangs up anything around here. When are you taking me home?"

Maeve holds the bra. It's at least three cup sizes bigger than anything her mother has ever worn. "Where did you get this, Ma?"

Her mother glares at her. "JC Penney. I bought it with my own good money. Why are you looking at me like that?"

"I think it got mixed up with someone else's laundry." Maeve folds the bra in half and sets it on the bed.

"Oh, no you don't," Effie says. She unlocks her brakes, peddles over, grabs the bra, and wheels herself back to the wardrobe.

Maeve hangs the bra, then all the bras in the drawer, many of which are marked with someone else's name.

Later, when Effie is at Bingo, Maeve will bring the bras to the nurses' station and ask him to return them to their rightful owners. The nurse, whose name is Jake, will take the bras like he's taking snakes from a sideshow.

39

Even after she knows what she should have known all along—
that her father and Anita have been having an affair—Maeve
uses the Cannon Sure Shot Anita Haverland gave her every
day, nearly every hour of every day. She threw away the film
Anita destroyed the day Maeve spied on her and Charlie, and
she hasn't seen Anita since. Still, as Maeve takes pictures of
her mother unpacking tomatoes from the grocery store, of her
peeling carrots for slaw, of her taking off her wedding ring so
she can moisturize her chapped hands, she can feel Anita's
approval. Maeve takes pictures of Stewart getting in and out
of his car, listening to his Walkman while mowing the lawn,
eating a chocolate-chip muffin for breakfast. Either he doesn't
notice her taking pictures, or he doesn't care. She takes pictures
of her father as he unloads boxes of smoke detectors from his
car for his new job at Fred's Safety & Prevention. When he
sees her, he stops, box heavy at his chest, and smiles.

"No, Dad, these are candids."

"What? You don't like my face?"

"Pretend I'm not here," Maeve says.

He carries the box into the house, but glances over his
shoulder at her, a grin like a weird clown on his face. He hates
his new job. Maeve heard her parents talking in the kitchen
when she was coming in for a snack. Effie said it was his own
fault for getting fired and he'd just have to live with the conse-
quences and Maeve felt bad for her father, and then worse for

feeling bad for him.

There's a part of Maeve that believes she'll show these pictures to Anita as some kind of peace offering. That Anita will realize Maeve has nothing to do with whatever is going on between her and Tom and Effie, that they can still be friends. Maeve has thought about sending her a note apologizing for lurking uninvited around her house and promising to never do it again, but she hasn't. Because what if she sends it and hears nothing back from Anita? It would mean Maeve never meant much of anything at all to her, that she was just—what? Part of some strategy game between her mother and Anita? Thinking about it makes her feel sick.

"You're making me nervous," Effie says one afternoon when Maeve hovers over her mother who bends to pick up a pile of dirt swept from the hall. There are bits of white hair from Clipper, sand they've tracked in from their cars, and a single dead ant that makes Maeve inexplicably sad. Who knows how far it strayed from its family, or how long it survived in this house?

Maeve holds the camera up to her mother's face. "No way," Effie says. She turns away so fast she nearly hits her head on the doorway.

"Why not?" Maeve asks.

"Take Collette's picture," her mother says.

"You're pretty, too," Maeve says, although she says this more out of loyalty than any real conviction. Her mother *can* be pretty when she does her hair and makeup and wears clothes that weren't purchased in nineteen-eighty, clothes in multiple shades of beige with giant shoulder pads. Pants with stirrups. It's nineteen-ninety-one and no one except Effie has hung onto those clothes. Occasionally, Maeve gets her mother to buy something more classic, like the red wool skirt that hangs in Effie's closet with the tags still attached.

Effie rolls her eyes. "Pretty like a goat."

"Mom," Maeve says, "Don't put yourself down. Besides, looks aren't everything." Maeve means this in the empowering way her friends have been talking about women not being objectified, but she can see by her mother's expression that she hasn't said the right thing the right way.

"If you say so," Effie says. She bends to sweep up the rest of the pile. "Make sure your homework is done by dinner time."

*****

And then, Maeve loses the Cannon Sure Shot. It's the last week of school and Maeve is positive she put the camera in her backpack. She had it out during her lunch period, when she took intentionally blurred pictures of everyone in their groups in the cafeteria. After that, it went back in the backpack and the backpack stayed with her until the fire drill when Maeve, in her panic, left the backpack under her desk.

Fire drills, even when she knows they're coming, make her nervous. She worries about the slipperiness of the stairs, the crush of bodies, the likelihood she'll mis-judge her footing and fall into Bianca Withers, who seems to always be right in front of her, and that the fall will cause Bianca to fall and then there'll be a heap of students, some of them bleeding, and that everyone will talk about how clumsy Maeve is, how oaf-like.

She didn't know this fire drill was coming. Which might mean it isn't a drill, because usually the principal announces drills over the loudspeaker. There could really be a fire somewhere. Why is everyone talking? Why aren't they moving with purpose? Why does everyone besides Maeve think nothing bad will ever happen to them?

Maeve makes it down the stairs and out the front door and then they all stand out there sweating and fanning themselves with their shirttails and Maeve suddenly realizes how badly she needs to pee. She presses her thighs together.

After all their heads are counted and they're allowed back in, Maeve beelines it to the bathroom. She gets back to the classroom just as Mrs. Garner is handing back their essays on "Freedom." Maeve reads through Mrs. Garner's comments to make sure she did a good job, which she did.

In the end, Maeve doesn't need to go into her backpack until she's in the car with her mother and wants her lip balm and then, when she realizes the camera is gone, she closes the backpack and closes her eyes.

"What's the matter?" Her mother asks.

"Just a headache," Maeve says. Maybe this is what she gets for keeping the camera even after her father got fired, even after her mother went to bed for a week and her father started sleeping on the couch. Even after Anita stopped calling Maeve, hasn't asked her to drop by, and has seemed to forget she ever existed.

The whole rest of the week is finals and it's not until Wednesday that she has a chance to go to the principal's office and report her missing camera. He mentions it over morning announcements, but no one ever comes forward.

Maeve doesn't see anyone with the camera that whole week, or the next school year. By then it doesn't matter because Maeve has finally accepted that Anita isn't going to invite her over ever again. Twice, Maeve has gone by the gallery where Anita's photographs were shown and both times there was nothing by A. Haverland there. The Haverlands still live in their big house, still drive their white cars, and Maeve still sees ads for Haverland Health with Anita's big smile and narrow waist. Her parents never talk about them anymore and when she mentions how weird it is to Stewart, he tells her to get over it.

40

Tom visits Effie every day at lunch. He sits with her while one of the aides feeds her. Nurse Jake tells Maeve this. "What do they talk about?" Maeve asks.

Jake shrugs. "They mostly just sit together. It's very sweet. I'll try to get a picture one of these days."

What Maeve wants is a tape recorder, but she doesn't think she can ask for that.

Maeve sits on Effie's bed and, instead of watching Judge Judy, she turns the TV off, eases her mother into a cardigan the color of bile that Maeve did not buy and has not seen, and unlocks her brakes. "How about a walk outside?"

Her mother plants her feet and tries to stand.

"A wheel," Maeve says, pushing her down gently. "I walk, you wheel."

"I can walk," Effie says.

"I know you can." Cindy the social worker has told Maeve to be "reinforcing rather than argumentative." Maeve finds the practice disconcerting, as if she's slipped back into her teenage years and is trying to get away with something. "Maybe it would be nice to just take a break, though," she says.

They walk and wheel through the hallway, into the elevator, down one floor. "Where are we going?" Effie asks.

"To get some fresh air," Maeve says.

The lobby is big and echo-y and Effie asks again, louder this time as though perhaps Maeve just didn't hear her the last time, "Where are we going?"

Ingrid waves from behind the reception desk. Into Effie's ear, Maeve says, "Just to get some fresh air."

Effie swats her away. "You don't have to drool all over me."

They're barely out the door when Effie says she's freezing. "Let's get in the sun," Maeve says.

"Why are you doing this to me?" Effie asks.

What's the point, really, of forcing her mother to be outside? Why not just let her be, even if being means sitting inside that cabbage-smelling room all day?

Maeve sighs. "It's April, Ma. The trees are starting to bloom." Only tiny buds, and still there are patches of snow in places that get a lot of shade. But, today is bright and this morning, Maeve saw a cardinal.

"That's no excuse," Effie says.

"You love spring."

At this, her mother plants her feet and Maeve almost doesn't stop her forward propulsion in time. Almost, Effie hurtles out of the wheelchair and onto her face. But Maeve stops and steadies herself. She congratulates herself on excellent reflexes. And then she starts to back up, turning the chair around so she can pull her mother instead of pushing her. "Okay," she says. "Let's head in."

But then, Effie tips her face up to the sun and sighs with contentment, as if none of their previous conversation happened. "This is nice."

Maeve drags a rattan chair next to her mother.

Maeve hasn't brought Clipper II today because he got neutered on Thursday and the vet said he needs to lay low. She misses patting him to keep her hands busy. She misses the sensation of not being alone. She takes her mother's hand and her mother doesn't pull away.

They're an hour later getting back to the room than Maeve planned because Effie falls asleep in the sun and Maeve dozes off, too, only for a minute or two, only until someone slams his car door and Maeve startles awake.

They're barely back in the room, Maeve still extracting her mother from the bile sweater, when the nurses' aide comes in with Effie's dinner tray. "Dinner, hon," she says and then she's gone in a flash of pink scrubs. Maeve didn't have time to say she thought Effie needed to be changed, soon if possible. She goes out to the nurses' station. "My Mom needs to be changed."

"Okay, hon," a different aide says. "Soon as we're done with dinner."

Maeve no longer gets the fluttery nerves of asking too much or too often or too strenuously. Instead, she feels the push of anger which she keeps locked behind her toothy smile. "How long will that be?" Maeve asks. "So that I can let my mother know."

Over her shoulder, the aide says, "Just a few, hon."

Maeve waits a moment to see if her presence will make them understand the urgency of not leaving her mother sitting in her own urine. But they ignore her with the steadiness of people well-practiced in the art of ignoring.

Back in the room, Maeve lifts the lid of her mother's dinner tray to reveal something pinkish, chopped, along with wet mashed potatoes, a dome of bright orange squash. Maeve dips her finger in the pink something, tastes. Salmon? Crab? In the hallway, she finds the menu taped to the nurses' station: Turkey Reuben. That, she would not have guessed.

She feeds her mother a bite of Reuben with some mashed potatoes. "What is it?" Her mother asks. She sticks out her tongue like a cat.

Maeve gets out the banana baby food she keeps in the night stand next to her mother's bed.

After Effie polishes off two jars, Maeve goes back into the hall. She's marching now, right up to the head nurse this time. "My mother has now been sitting in urine for an hour," Maeve says. Whatever her mother has done, isn't this a fate worse than prison?

The nurse looks up. The red lining his eyes suggests he's exhausted or drunk. He says, "Why didn't you say something sooner?"

When Maeve gets back to the room, Effie picks at a drop of dried banana baby food on her shirt. "Are we eating?"

"You ate," Maeve says.

"You have me mixed up with someone else. Can I have a sandwich?"

Maeve pivots with sudden urgency. "Why not?"

At the nurses' station, Maeve asks for tuna on white bread for her mother, extra mayonnaise, no crusts. "I can cut the crusts off myself," she says, aware that her makeup is all over her face and her eyes are leaking tears and she must seem like an insane person.

"We can put it in the blender," the nurse says.

"Then it won't be a sandwich," Maeve says.

He nods. "You understand your mother could aspirate—"

"I'll be careful," Maeve says. "Small bites, lots of chewing. Sips of water in between."

When she gets back with the sandwich, Effie smiles widely. "I was just thinking about a sandwich!"

Maeve hands Effie one square of sandwich after another and watches her chew and reminds her to chew it good and offers her sips of room-temperature coffee in between. She's thinking about how Paige won't ever feed her like this because she doesn't deserve it.

Effie inhales and then coughs and coughs and coughs.

Wendy-in-her-head asks her why she didn't listen to Jake and Maeve asks Wendy if she's ever wanted to be a better person.

Better than what? Wendy asks.

The coughing isn't alarming at first, and Maeve doesn't ring the bell because she's always ringing the bell to say her mother needs to use the ladies' room or would like to lie down or get up or be changed or have a drink of water. She's just going to wait this out.

It's Raine who pops her head in first. "Oh," she says, and then she pops out and is replaced by Jake who has a machine with him.

"She can't be choking because she's coughing," Maeve says, which is what her mother always said. And yet Jake is back with the machine with a clear container the size of a small aquarium. There's a tube, and Maeve doesn't have time for a better look because Jake bumps her out of the way. In seconds he has the tube up her mother's nose and down her throat and within a minute the sandwich that had been sucked into her lung is sucked back out.

Effie looks stunned but unharmed. Maeve thanks Jake who nods and wheels his machine out and mercifully doesn't say anything to reprimand Maeve. "I'll puree it next time," Maeve says. "Or bring pudding."

Jake nods again.

"Soft foods," Maeve says. Her legs tremble.

"Thickened liquids," Jake says.

"What?" Maeve shakes her head. "Is that new? Is that something new?" By "new" she means worse. Of course it is.

Maeve gets home earlier than usual because she can't stand to stay in her mother's room with the smell of wet bread and sweat, even if it's her own sweat. She doesn't want to waste the day, and so she finds Paige in her room and suggests they go dress shopping for Paige's Sophomore Semi-formal.

"I'm not going to the dance," Paige says. "So, there's no point in getting a dress."

"You don't need a date. Girls can go with just a group of friends, right?"

"I don't want to go. Period."

"You might change your mind and then you'll have nothing to wear

"I won't change my mind."

"Please," Maeve says. Wendy-in-her-head is giving her a look that demands an explanation, but Maeve ignores her. "You can drive," Maeve says, dangling the keys to her Toyota as if it's a sports car and driving to the mall is some rare treat.

Paige stares at her.

"Just get a dress and then you'll have it in case you decide to go." The sound of her mother being suctioned is still playing in her head and Maeve needs to replace it with the rustle of satin. "Please," Maeve says. "For me." Since she hatched this plan in the car on the way home from Mild Brook, she can't let go of the image of them at Macy's, sliding their fingers over ruched bodices and laced edges and exclaiming over midnight purple or mermaid green. She has imagined Paige preening in front of a mirror, and Maeve telling her she's beautiful and smart, because it's important to be both, even though smart has nothing to do with this particular excursion, and then taking her to get the right bra for the dress because that is something a mother knows from experience can be the most important part. She'll end up spending more on the bra than on the dress, but that's okay because a good bra is foundational.

When Paige says nothing, Maeve says, "I want to cheer you up."

Paige snorts. "I need way more than cheering up."

Obviously, this is where Maeve is supposed to ask what Paige needs, but what Paige needs is very likely something Maeve cannot deliver.

Paige stands. "Fine."

In Macy's, Paige heads directly for the black cap-sleeved sequined floor-length dress. It's fitted like a potato sack. The only thing that makes it not maternal is the sequins. Maeve holds up a hot pink strapless with a fitted waist. "No way," Paige says.

She's hardly even looked at it, so Maeve carries it around with them, although in truth, Maeve doesn't know what she likes about the dress and ignores Wendy-in-her-head when she asks what she's doing. Maeve chooses an electric blue chiffon with a slit to the thigh, a lime green with an open back, a fitted silver sheath.

"Mom," Paige says. "I'm not a hooker."

This makes Maeve recoil. She hadn't meant it that way. Of course she hadn't meant it that way. Wendy asks her to consider why she's over-sexualizing her traumatized daughter and Maeve says she wants Paige to feel beautiful. She's picking dresses that will highlight her creamy skin. And the fact that they're skimpy—well, Maeve can't answer that. "Can't or won't," Wendy asks, and Maeve closes her eyes.

"These are nice dresses," Maeve says. But she can feel their near-nakedness burning her forearms. She puts them all on a rack that holds coats and they look like clowns at a funeral.

One afternoon when Maeve was fourteen or fifteen, Anita let her try on the backless green dress she wore to her gallery opening. They were in Anita's bedroom, which had plush white carpet and a thick white bedspread and a million pillows—all white and cream—in different textures. Maeve went into the bathroom with the dress and when she came out, Anita zipped her up. In the mirror, Maeve stood as tall as she could, the dress like nothing she'd ever felt against her skin. "You look stunning," Anita said. And she did. Somehow, even though she was shorter and chubbier than Anita, she really did look stunning. She smiled so hard her cheeks hurt.

And now, remembering that, Maeve starts to cry.

"Ma?" Paige's face is lit with worry but Maeve can't stop crying.

"I loved her," Maeve says. "I loved her, too."

Paige doesn't ask who Maeve means. She rubs her back in circles, like Maeve did when she was little, like Effie did for Maeve. Maeve cries for a long time. Two sales people—one an old woman with short gray hair who could be in the room next to Effie but isn't, the other a girl so young and pale Maeve thinks she's the child of a vampire—scurry over to ask if she's alright, if she needs anything. Maeve shakes her head. Paige says, kindly, that her mother just needs a minute. A different daughter would go wait in the car, but Paige stays rooted in place, rubbing Maeve's back until she's all cried out.

In the end, Paige insists on the black dress, which doesn't need a special bra. It makes Paige look like a forty-year-old librarian at her coworker's second wedding, but Maeve says it looks nice. Maeve takes her—practically drags her—to the shoe store where Paige picks out the first pair of heels she tries on, which are plain black pumps. Not even with a buckle.

On the way home, Maeve is mostly silent as Paige navigates through traffic blurred by headlights and streetlights. "Can you see okay?" Maeve asks only once when it appears Paige is about to drive over the raised median.

"Do you want to drive?" Paige asks.

She does, but Maeve knows better than to say so. Wendy congratulates her.

Maeve unbuckles her seatbelt. "That was fun, wasn't it?" When Paige shrugs, Maeve smiles harder, even though her dried tears crack like plaster on her cheeks.

"My mother never did anything like this with me," Maeve says, following close behind Paige as they mount the front steps.

And then she remembers being with her mother in JC Penney and her mother holding up the purple plaid overalls with the teal blue sweater and telling Maeve it looked "sharp" and Maeve saying no one said that anymore and her mother smiling so hard Maeve could see the cracks in the foundation around her lips.

41

Stewart says mildly that he should come see Effie, but it's a non-offer, really, because he follows the offer with the statement that he and Natalie have had to sell their boat. "Things are tight here," he says, "But, I can put the flight on a credit card if you think I should."

Then he says, "She probably won't even know me. I'm not sure I could handle that."

Maeve almost hangs up on him because, really, what does he know, tucked away in the glory of California sun, one Christmas visit a year. He witnessed only briefly the deep slide into dementia, hears the thinness of Effie's voice when she manages to speak into the phone when he calls, takes pleasure in the fact that she usually remembers him by his voice.

Maeve says, "I'm sorry to hear that." And then she half-listens as Stewart complains about the price of gas and food and electricity. She even makes sympathetic noises so she can tell Wendy she was polite throughout the conversation

When Stewart finishes with his excuses, Maeve says, "You have to do what you feel is right." She hangs up feeling righteous.

Maeve makes ham and scalloped potatoes and glazed carrots. She bakes cream puffs from scratch and fills them with a delicate cream filling she remakes eight times before it isn't watery or stiff as concrete. She buys lilies and yellow and pink tulips and sets out three vases of them. She has purchased one of those paper-letter signs and strings it in the doorway between the kitchen and living room. If they aren't careful, they might hang themselves on "Happy Mother's Day!"

At Mild Brook, she eases her mother into the new butter-yellow cardigan she's bought for her and tucks a blanket around her lap, not thinking she'll have to untuck it to get her into the car. At the nurses' station, Maeve signs her mother out.

"Happy Mother's Day," Jake says.

Maeve swallows against the glug of tears in her throat. This morning, Paige gave her a tiny framed photograph of her hand and Paige's intertwined. The day Paige took it, Maeve had been trying all day to give Effie a shower and she wouldn't take her clothes off and Paige said she needed Maeve for just a minute, just one hand. Maeve had said to make it quick and Paige took her hand, twined her fingers through Maeve's, and took the picture. Maeve had forgotten all about it.

Maeve wheels her mother out to the car, bumps the wheelchair down backwards over the curbside. "What are you doing to me?" Her mother asks.

"I'm taking you home," Maeve says.

"What do you call this?" Effie waves an arm elaborately at Mild Brook.

Maeve starts to cry in earnest, tears sluicing down her face onto her mother's lap as she does up the seatbelt. How does she still have any tears left, after all the crying she's been doing?

"You'll ruin your makeup," Effie says.

Maeve laughs. Last night she said to Peter, "I'm not doing such a good job of this."

And Peter said, "You're doing the best you can." Maeve hated him a little for not saying something more, something better.

Now, Peter meets her in the driveway and they wrestle her mother out of the car, with as much care as possible. Effie's body feels like a sack of bones and Maeve tells Peter to slow down, slow down before they break something.

He is gentle, though, and practiced, and Maeve reminds herself that he often helps his clients on and off with their jackets and sneakers and mittens.

When Peter and Tom have brought everything to the table, Maeve cuts her mother's ham into very small cubes. Miniscule, as if for a doll, for a tea party. Still. Effie takes a bite of biscuit and coughs. "She's not choking," Maeve says. And she's not. She's fine, she's okay. She drinks from the coffee which Maeve has served lukewarm.

Clipper II sniffs around for crumbs and Maeve coaxes him to her mother, eases his head into her lap. "Clipper wants to say hi," Maeve says.

She takes her mother's hand and places it on Clipper's back. Her mother strokes the dog. "He's cute. What did you say his name was again?"

"Clipper." Maeve's breath feels like she's just finished running up the stairs with the laundry.

Her mother smiles and coos. "We had a dog named Clipper."

It seems ridiculous to try to convince her mother this dog is that dog, to confuse her when she's not confused. "We did," Maeve says.

"That dog was a good dog," her father says.

"Until you weren't watching him and he got hit by a car." Wendy gives Maeve a hard look, but Maeve feels delighted by her meanness, by the shock on her father's face. If she can't blame him for Anita's death, at least she has this.

"That's terrible," Effie says.

Biscuit midway to his mouth, her father says, "I wasn't even home when Clipper got hit."

Maeve laughs. "Yes, you were. You and Charlie and Anita were working on a presentation and you were supposed to be watching him and he got out."

"No," her father says, chewing now, bits of biscuit stuck to his lips. "I remember your Mom calling me, hysterical, because he'd gotten out. I was at the office. We might have been working on a presentation, but I wasn't home."

"I'm sure she was hysterical, but it was you who called her." As Maeve says this, there's a flicker of some half-remembered memory: her mother running into the street, her mother bent over Clipper.

Now, her mother picks up a scalloped potato with her fingers, cream sauce dripping down her wrist, and onto her lap. She feeds the potato to Clipper, II. "He's a good boy."

"I wasn't home," her father says. His words are clear and dry and Maeve realizes he's telling the truth. It makes her dizzy to touch the memory of her father being there when Clipper ran into the street and then touch the other memory—the one of the person running, crying, momentarily not-watching, being her mother.

Of course, this is where Maeve is supposed to apologize. She's been in therapy long enough to recognize an opportunity when she sees one. She looks at her father and the words are right there, rolling around on her tongue, but she thinks of her father and Anita Haverland backlit by the firelight that day twenty-five years ago and she remembers that at least some of her anger is justified. Unless that, too, is a faulty memory.

What would it feel like to forgive him? Wendy-in-her-head asks.

I don't know who I'd be, Maeve says.

Maeve stuffs a slice of ham into her mouth and chews until someone changes the subject.

When they've all eaten more than they should, Maeve and Paige clear the plates while Peter plays rummy with her mother and Tom watches. They bring out the cream puffs and decaf coffee and Effie says she's full. "I'd like to go home," she says.

Maeve's heart becomes a fist and knocks hard against her ribcage. How will she explain to her mother that her home isn't her home anymore?

Her father shakes his head. He says, "She means home to the nursing home."

"No she doesn't," Maeve says.

But now her mother is pushing herself away from the table and Maeve has locked the brakes on her wheelchair so she's practically pushing herself over.

"I took her for a walk in the parking lot last week and she asked to go home and I explained about the house." He shakes his head. "There I was, feeling really bad about selling and then she pointed to the building and said 'There.'"

"I don't believe you," Maeve says, even though she does.

He shrugs. "Suit yourself."

Maybe she needs to go to the bathroom and so Maeve wheels her down the hall and wrestles her into the bathroom that has never felt narrow before but does now. She gets her mother's pants down and gets her situated on the toilet and Effie asks, "What are you doing to me?" but then she pees and Maeve hands her toilet paper and Effie hands it back to

Maeve when she's done with it.

Maeve uses hand sanitizer on her mother's hands because she can't make her mother's hands reach the sink from the wheelchair without dislocating her shoulders. Then she washes her own hands. She takes her back to the table and cuts a cream puff in half and puts it on a plate that used to be her mother's—one that went with a tea cup with tiny yellow flowers. Effie says, "I already had one," and pushes the plate away.

"You didn't," Maeve says.

Peter gives her a look and she knows she should let it go, but she says, "It took me half a day to make these because they're you've favorite." Wendy-in-her-head asks her what she's trying to accomplish here.

Effie pats her hair. "You're a good girl."

No one else says anything, but Maeve can feel them staring at her. She knows they think she's lost it, and she's pretty sure she has.

Finally, Effie says, "Can you take me home now?"

Tom gives Maeve a look. "Fine," Maeve says. "Fine."

Tom and Peter help get her in the car and Peter says he'll drive her back even though Maeve says she can do it. But they both know she can't do it. That she'd cry the whole way there and the whole way back. She'd cry so much her eyes would swell and she wouldn't be able to see and someone would have to come and get her.

"Thank you," Maeve says to Peter. He leans down and kisses her and she kisses him back.

Inside, Tom helps Paige clear the table and pack up the leftovers and Maeve leans against the counter watching them until Paige says, "Go take a nap, Ma. We'll finish in here."

Maeve can't remember the last time she's napped, but

suddenly she's so exhausted she can hardly stand. She mumbles a thank you, makes her way down the hall, and falls onto the bed which Peter made with fresh sheets this morning. She leaves the door open and, for the few moments before she falls asleep, she listens to Paige and Tom talk about the biscuits (should they give them to the birds or will they last another few days?), the ham (Paige will take some for lunches), the cream puffs (tomorrow, her father will bring two to her mother). Clipper pushes open the door and hops onto the bed and Maeve curls herself around him.

A while later she hears Paige come in and stand in the doorway. Maeve keeps her eyes closed. For a long time, Maeve can feel Paige standing there and she suspects Paige can tell she's awake. And then Maeve feels the air change, feels Paige climb onto the bed, feels her daughter tuck herself beside her.

Acknowledgements

Thanks to everyone at Apprentice House for helping me make this book what it is. It's a great gift to work with people who are as enthusiastic about my work as I am!

As always, thanks to my writing cohort: Elisha Emerson, Melanie Brooks, and Jess Pulver. Without their steady encouragement, this book would not have made it into this iteration. Thanks also to Kate Kaminski for her close reading, thoughtful feedback, and unfailing encouragement.

Thanks to my parents, Frances and Francis, for being proud of me.

Thanks especially to my husband, Steve, for his unwavering support and constant belief in me.

About the Author

Jen Dupree is an assistant editor for *The Masters Review*, a librarian, and a former bookstore owner. She has an MFA in Creative Writing from USM's Stonecoast program. Her work has appeared in *December*, *Solstice*, *The Masters Review*, *On the Rusk* and other notable places. She is the winner of the Writer's Digest Fiction Contest for 2017, and a two-time winner of a Maine Literary Award (2022, 2006). Her novel, *The Miraculous Flight of Owen Leach* was published in April of 2022 by Apprentice House Press.

Apprentice
House Press
Loyola University Maryland

Apprentice House is the country's only campus-based, student-staffed book publishing company. Directed by professors and industry professionals, it is a nonprofit activity of the Communication Department at Loyola University Maryland.

Using state-of-the-art technology and an experiential learning model of education, Apprentice House publishes books in untraditional ways. This dual responsibility as publishers and educators creates an unprecedented collaborative environment among faculty and students, while teaching tomorrow's editors, designers, and marketers.

Eclectic and provocative, Apprentice House titles intend to entertain as well as spark dialogue on a variety of topics. Financial contributions to sustain the press's work are welcomed. Contributions are tax deductible to the fullest extent allowed by the IRS.

To learn more about Apprentice House books or to obtain submission guidelines, please visit www.apprenticehouse.com.

Apprentice House Press
Communication Department
Loyola University Maryland
4501 N. Charles Street
Baltimore, MD 21210
Ph: 410-617-5265
info@apprenticehouse.com • www.apprenticehouse.com

www.ingramcontent.com/pod-product-compliance
Lightning Source LLC
Chambersburg PA
CBHW051336020726
47501CB00007B/2115